Pe

Book 3 in the Blended Blessings Series
by
CaSandra McLaughlin & Michelle Stimpson

Acknowledgments from
CaSandra McLaughlin

I thank and praise God for His many blessings. Special thanks to Michelle Stimpson my mentor, prayer partner and friend. Thanks for pushing me daily, Michelle. It's because of you that I made it through this process. Words can't express how grateful I am. Love you, sis.

Thanks to my #1 fan, my husband, Richard for all of your love and support. Thanks to my baby girl, Chloe, you are my why. Life will deal you several cards but it's up to you how you play them. I pray that how I've played my cards will inspire and encourage you to succeed in life.

Last, but certainly not least, thanks to all of the many readers who have allowed the Holley family to be a part of your reading world. Thanks for all of the reviews, posts, and inbox messages. I love you all. Thanks a million!!

Acknowledgments from
Michelle Stimpson

All Glory and Honor to The Most High! I'm grateful to the Lord for His faithfulness!

Thank you to all the readers, family, and friends, who have supported this series. I think I've made some new family members in Marshall, TX! It's my pleasure to connect with so many people through writing!

Shout-out to Gretchen Davis for sharing your expertise about senior living centers.

Thank-you to my immediate family for loaning me out to write! I never take for granted that you all are there for me, even when you're kind of gone.

Finally, thanks to CaSandra for partnering with me and reminding me how fun it is to collaborate. The Blended Blessings Series has indeed been a blessing to me!

Dedications

From Michelle Stimpson:
For the growing family of Christ.
It gets tough sometimes, but it would be even tougher without the hope of Christ.

From CaSandra McLaughlin:
For all the aspiring writers:
Don't dream about it, write about it.

Chapter 1

Since my first two attempts to host a gathering at our new house failed miserably thanks to my husband's ex-wife the first time and my mother-in-law the second time, I decided to try hosting a private family outing elsewhere. Maybe the Holleys needed to bond with ourselves first. Maybe our house was just for living, and we did plenty of it there with seven people—me, my husband and his twin daughters from a previous marriage as well as my son and daughter from two previous marriages and now my grandson. Ours could have been the poster-family for blended families, we had so much going on.

It wasn't just the kids, though. Seemed like the adults had just as much blending to do as the juveniles. And sometimes I wondered who was doing a better job.

If I wasn't busy trying to figure out a way to keep peace with my husband's baggage, I was trying to calm my own, including my son Demarcus's father. Since Darren and I had moved into our spacious home in the quaint town of Lancing Springs, TX, Demarcus's dad, Marcus Jackson, was filling my baby's head with fantasies. He had gone so far as to buy Demarcus a cell phone so they could keep in touch without my interference.

Darren and I decided to keep the phone in our possession, but that proved a nuisance because poor Demarcus always wanted to check and see if his father had sent him a text. After praying, we finally just put some safeguards on the phone and then gave it to Demarcus, which turned out to be the best thing because Marcus didn't even pay the bill on time. That phone would be off a week and on a week.

I should have known the man wasn't going to pay an extra bill on the regular. Shoot, he'd never given me anything toward Demarcus's care. He sure wasn't about to pay toward an "extra" for our son.

Nonetheless, Marcus called two days before my carefully planned family trip to Big Wolf Lodge, an indoor waterpark resort about an hour north. We had already booked and paid for the largest suite possible, with a master bedroom, a kids' room, and a family room so that everyone could have their space. From what I'd seen online, our family was headed for a wonderful weekend.

When I saw Marcus's number on my cell phone, I closed my Bible and took a deep breath while sitting at the kitchen table. Miss Earlene had warned me that I shouldn't even take a phone into my private prayer time. I should have listened to her because seeing some people's names on the phone screen could bring an end to all sense of peace and tranquility.

"Yes, Marcus?"

"Well, hello, there. And how are you on this fine summer day?"

"I'm blessed. And you?" I forced myself to ask.

"Missing my son. And his mother."

"Why do you always have to do this?"

"Do what?"

"Flirt," I said. "I'm happily married, Marcus. You and I will never be together again. Never. *Ever.* So you can stop telling me how much you miss me. Now, what would you like to discuss regarding our *son?*"

Marcus breathed heavily, as though he had to cool off.

That makes two of us.

"We can't co-parent effectively with all this hostility between us. It's not good for Demarcus," my ex tried to lecture.

"It wasn't good for Demarcus to be living off one parent's wages, either, but he's done that for most of his life. Next."

"Why you always gotta bring up the past?"

I squeezed my eyes shut tight and tried to analyze this conversation for what it was. Marcus was baiting me, trying to pull me into an argument like a bill collector trying to set up a payment arrangement with somebody whose account is already in the negative. *Lord, You said You would give me wisdom when I ask for it. I need you raaaat now.*

Marcus asked, "You still there?"

"Yes. I'm here. What do you want?"

"I want to take Demarcus with me to my nephew's graduation."

"Who's graduating and when?"

"Dinky. April's son. Finishing from Texas Southern University with a degree in engineering. This weekend."

No way is he taking my baby all the way down to Houston. "That's great for Dinky and April. If you send me an address, I'll send him a gift. But Demarcus isn't free. We've got a family outing planned."

"The graduation is a family outing with *me*. And you know how I feel about education. This is important; I want Demarcus to see some achievement on my side of the family."

How many people on your side of the family can even spell achievement? I swallowed my laugh. "I, too, value education, but you can't call us on Thursday and expect me to rearrange my life to accommodate your last-minute plans."

"Oh. So it's about *you*, huh? I thought we were talking about what's best for *Demarcus*?"

He was about to summon "old girl" in me—the dead person I was before I had a little Bible-study in me. "Listen, if you want to pull out calendars and schedule some things in advance, I am more than willing to work with you. But I'm sorry, the tickets for our weekend have already been purchased."

Well, in a way they had. The truth was: Once we'd reserved the most spacious family floor plan, the waterpark tickets were included. Our expenses would be the same whether Demarcus joined us or not. But Marcus didn't need to know that.

"So you just gonna deprive me of an opportunity to see my son?" he snapped at me.

"You deprived yourself, Marcus."

He snickered. "All this talk about you being blessed, taking my son to church. You just like the rest of the church hypocrites."

"A hypocrite?" I seethed, scooting my Bible clear to the right on the table. "You got a lot of nerve." I won't even repeat the words I spoke to Marcus because they were far from godly. Matter of fact, they were far from lady-like but he *took* me there! I mean, he turned on the ignition, switched the gear to drive, and put the pedal to the metal with his accusations. Had we been on a reality TV show, there would have been nothing but a string of *Bleep! Bleep! Bleeps!* heard as we argued.

I was so far gone—I had traveled from the kitchen all the way to the family room arguing—I didn't even hear the twins come through the front door after school.

As soon as I had my last few choice words and hung up the phone with Marcus, I turned and saw Tyler facing me with her eyes wide open and her mouth nearly on the floor.

"Miss Angelia! Dang! You just went *platinum* on somebody!" She smiled and offered me some dap.

Shaking my head and sighing, I pushed her fist down. "I shouldn't have done that, Tyler."

"But Miss Angelia! You gotta start doing that more often! My Momma says you can't hold it in when you get mad at somebody or else you'll explode and have a heart attack! That's what happened to my other granny."

"I thought Marcy's mother died of a stroke."

"Same thing."

"No. It's not. And please don't go telling everybody about my temporary insanity, okay?"

Tyler nodded, still wearing a silly grin. "Your secret's safe with me. And God. He's the One you gotta talk to, you know?"

"Yes, I know." Forgive me, Lord.

I ventured to put my arm around her shoulder as we walked back to the kitchen. I counted it a blessing that she didn't shrug me off.

Tyler always raided the pantry and refrigerator when she got off the bus. Those summer academic camp sack lunches did little to satisfy her appetite.

"Skylar went to the room?"

"Yeah. She's doin' the poor-little-rich-girl-run-upstairs 'cause this girl named Alexis who cheated made a higher grade on the Algebra test," Tyler divulged while pouring a glass of orange juice.

"How do y'all know Alexis cheated?"

"'Cause first of all she ain't that smart. Second, she had the formulas written right on her hands. Skylar wanted to tell the teacher, but I told her not to be no snitch. That girl gon' get hers one day. But for right now, Skylar's worried about getting the high achievement award for the summer camp."

"Are you concerned about your scores?" I asked.

"Naaah. I know I'm smart. I don't need tests and grades and teachers to tell me that."

"Well…that's certainly one way of looking at it."

She took another gulp of juice, then became suddenly still. Her nose wrinkled. "It's too quiet. Where is everybody?"

"Demarcus is over at Miss Earlene's shooting hoops with Cameron. Your dad is at the gym. Amber took Dylan for his check-up."

"And here you are. All alone. Goin' left on people." She squinted at me. "What else do you do when we're not here?"

"Go on, Tyler." I swatted at her arm. "Get started on your homework."

She giggled. "I'm just sayin'!"

I suppose if I had to lose my composure in front of a child, I'd rather it be Tyler than anyone else. She always kept it real, even when real was ugly. Tyler was the one who sounded the alarm when her mother's boyfriend, Elroy, tried to take advantage of Skylar. And it was Tyler who told on Marcy when she reunited with Elroy. Tyler had a mouth on her, but more often than not, her outspoken intelligence worked in her favor.

The postal carrier ran early in the summer—or maybe I just checked it earlier, I wasn't sure. Anyway, with the arrival of the girls' bus, I walked down my driveway to get the mail.

Most of it was junk. But there was one from the Office of the Attorney General addressed to Amber. With no regard for federal laws, I tore through the envelope and read that J.D. had requested a paternity test for my grandson, Dylan.

More bleeps ran through my head as I realized that my daughter was headed down the same messes-with-the-exes road I'd been traveling on since I was nineteen.

Lord, help us all.

Chapter 2

Finally. After a weekend at an indoor waterpark, two weekends of summer academic camp activities, I could look forward to a weekend alone with just me and my husband to celebrate our one-year anniversary. Well, it wasn't an entire weekend—just Saturday night. But I was determined to make it special and make it last for as long as possible while the twins were with their mother, Demarcus had been requested to spend the weekend with his father for an alleged birthday party, and Amber was preparing to take Dylan to visit my cousins in Marshall, TX. She didn't really want to go, but when she saw how excited I was about having the house clear of little ones, she graciously suggested that I let her use the truck so she could spend time with Claudia and Erica.

My first thought was "no" because I'm kind of particular about my grandson.

Dylan was only eight months old. He weighed sixteen pounds and had a contagious, toothless grin that could melt a snowman in ten seconds flat. He had to be the cutest baby in the whole state.

I sat on the guest chair in Amber's room, bouncing Dylan on my knee as she packed their bags for the weekend. "I still think we should enter his picture in a contest."

"Mom, we're not going to make him a pageant boy."

"I'm not saying put him in pageants, but he is absolutely adorable," I sang as Dylan smiled and drool came falling from his lips. I dabbed his mouth with his *I Love Granny* bib. "Plus he could win money for college scholarships with some of the contests."

"What did *Dad* say about putting Dylan in a beauty contest?" she asked.

I rolled my eyes. "I haven't said anything to him about it."

Amber laughed. "Yeah, right, because you know he's not going to let us put Dylan in a pageant. He's already started looking at football camps for pre-k kids."

I had to admit to myself: Amber was right. Darren already had dreams of both Demarcus and Dylan following in his footsteps, playing professional football. Demarcus liked football well enough, yet he preferred basketball and soccer. He wasn't really good at any sport, but he enjoyed playing with his teammates. He wasn't nearly as serious about it as Darren had been at that age.

But Darren had started whispering NFL-sweet-nothings into Dylan's ears at the hospital when he was born. This boy was headed for the football field—no pageants allowed.

"Oh well. At least he'll be an *attractive* football star like his grandpa."

I helped Amber carry the bags downstairs and loaded them into my SUV. "You remember the way?"

Amber huffed. "Yes, mother. It's a straight shot to Marshall."

"You got the land line number to Claudia's, too?"

"Yes, ma'am."

"Okay. Turn on the ignition. I want to make sure there's enough gas in the car."

Amber followed my direction, which ended in a showing of the tank being more than half full. "Stop and fill it up."

"Mom. We're going to make it to Marshall with no problem. Gas is probably cheaper there, anyway."

"You're right. Well, the triple-A card is in the glove compartment," I reminded her, strapping my precious grandson in his car seat.

"Okay, enough already. You and Dad enjoy your weekend." She pressed the garage door opener.

A flood of sunshine entered as she put the car in reverse. "See you Sunday afternoon."

"Okay. And call and check on Demarcus while you're there. I know he's riding back with you, but I'm saying—just in case he needs anything."

"Yes, Mom. We're leaving now. Step away from the vehicle."

I gave a fake grin. "Very funny, Amber."

Nonetheless, I shuffled backward and watched as she and my grandson departed. Worry gripped my heart, so I prayed even as they drove out of sight. "Lord, protect them according to Psalm 91." We had studied that chapter in the women's group. I recalled the first verse and remembered that I was the "he" who abided under the shadow of the Almighty, where there is the only safety we can ever know.

With my mind calmed by the scriptures, I pressed the button to lower the garage door and walked back into the house. The empty house. The house that my husband would return to in about an hour.

I had things to do: take a shower, get my smell-good on, order our favorite Mexican dishes for dinner. I called in the food to Papa Villalba's Cantina restaurant and sent Darren a text reminding him to pick it up on his way home. He responded: "Can't wait."

A smile covered my face as I double-timed it upstairs in preparation for our peaceful, wonderful anniversary night. We

16

had considered going to a hotel for a staycation but decided instead that our mini-mansion was just as beautiful as any Marriott. If we could just get the kids out, we'd be able to enjoy our space even more.

Now that we were finally going to be alone, I had a change of heart once I stepped out of the shower. *Forget that silk nightgown.* I was going to wear my birthday suit instead. *Isn't this what being married and living in your own house is all about?*

I dried off, applied oil to my soft skin, reapplied my lipstick and pulled my hair into a messy ponytail. I glanced at my body in the full-length mirror on the back of the bathroom door. Sure, I had my pudgy parts, but Darren wouldn't mind. He loved every inch of me—even the extra inches—and I was ready to show him how much I appreciated him, too. We'd been through a lot in our first year of marriage. *We deserve what's getting ready to go down tonight!*

But before I could greet my husband wearing nothing at all, I had to throw on a robe and double-check every window to make sure we wouldn't end up on YouTube.

After my window-check, I got a text from Darren. Still waiting with a few of the kids. Miscommunication about time. Parents running late.

I screamed, "Really?!"

My husband and his football players could really get on my last nerve. Plus, these boys were big and burly. They could handle themselves. Shoot, they could all walk home as far as I was concerned. Darren, however, was a stickler for making sure the boys were supervised as much as possible to ward off foolishness.

How much longer??????

Not long. Parents are on the way.

What was supposed to be "not long" ended up being ninety minutes. While my husband was playing babysitter, I was in our bedroom waiting, fuming, and looking out my window hoping every car that approached the corner was his.

By the time my husband arrived, I was almost through. But somehow I caught a glance of the diamond on my hand and remembered that this was my anniversary. *I'm happily married. I'm in love with a wonderful man. The house is empty. I'm still naked under this robe and Darren can be naked in about three seconds.*

Although my attitude still wanted to be funky, my spirit and my body were telling me to get over it. So I did. And as soon as my husband pulled into the driveway, I pulled the belt on my robe and let it fall to the floor.

I walked out of our bedroom. Darren was coming up the staircase to meet me. His eyes traveled my body and his sexy smirk covered his face. "Baby, I'm so sorry it took so long. I'll make it worth the wait."

I folded my arms behind his neck. "I'm gonna hold you to it."

Just then, I felt his phone buzz in his pocket.

"Do. Not. Answer. That," I said, thinking it had to be Coach Minden or someone else on the coaching staff.

Without looking at the screen, he took the phone out of his pocket and tossed it to the floor. "Whoever it is, they can wait," he agreed. He kissed my neck gently. I backpedaled to our bedroom.

We had just laid on the bed when suddenly my phone began to buzz. Darren's phone buzzed again, too, and we both realized something was happening. We both sighed while taking a break to check phones. My eyes bugged wide when I saw the words from Tyler: My momma apartment on fire! Tell my daddy to call me! I hadn't even processed the words when Darren yelled, "I gotta go! Something happened at Marcy's."

"I'm coming with you."

Darren rushed down the stairs to head to the car.

My heart raced as I scrambled to find undergarments, clothes, and shoes. Darren blew the horn a few seconds later. I grabbed my purse and met him outside. He sped off before I had my seatbelt snapped.

"Did she text you again? Are they okay? Did everyone get out?" I asked.

"Yeah. But they've lost everything," he said. Darren was hunched over the steering, driving like a mad man. "Whole unit had to be evacuated."

"Thank God nobody's hurt."

The previous times we'd gone to Marcy's apartment took us about fifteen minutes. That night, it took us seven. As we approached the complex, fire trucks, police cars, and an ambulance blocked the entrance. Darren parked along the curb, activated his hazards, and hopped out. I followed him up to the nearest police officer.

"Officer, my name is Darren Holley. My daughters are residents here. I need to check on them."

"Holley, eh?" the officer said, peering into my husband's face. "You the football coach at the main high school?"

"Yes, sir."

For once, I was glad everyone in town knew my husband.

"Well, congratulations. And don't worry. We've got everything under control here. Nobody's hurt. A few folks had smoke inhalation. We got 'em some oxygen and they're fine. Had one person kinda unruly. She's sittin' in the back of the squad car over there." He pointed at one of their vehicles. "We're taking her in until she sobers up."

"Yes, but my daughters. I need to see them."

Darren hadn't bothered to follow the officer's hand, but I did. I recognized the bushy weave right away as Marcy's.

"Daddy! Daddy!"

We turned to see Tyler and Skylar running through the maze of emergency responders. Skylar, of course, was a little slower because her legs were still not quite one hundred percent since her car accident.

Tyler was first to reach her father and immediately she spilled the beans, "Daddy, Momma had some candles. And she went to sleep. She was drunk. And she burned our whole apartment down!"

"Honey, are you sure she was drunk?" Darren asked.

"She was," Skylar cosigned. "Daddy, it was terrible. The fire...it was everywhere. Just like a scary movie."

Darren looked at me like I might have some answers. All I could say was, "Babe, she's the one in the back of the police car."

All Darren and I could do was stand there holding the girls, trying to shield their eyes from the horror of watching their mother's apartment burn, seeing their neighbors outside draped in blankets, listening to the cries of people who were losing everything that belonged to them except their very lives.

We soon learned that what the fire didn't destroy, the firemen soaked to death with their water hoses and fire extinguishers. The apartment was a total loss. I'd never been so glad that the girls had moved some of their things to our house. Still, the photo albums and records were destroyed. Stuffed animals. Memories of the days when their parents were still together. Gone.

Both the girls were too tired and distraught to say much on the way back to our house. Upon arrival, I noticed the light on upstairs in Amber's room. I checked my phone and saw that both Amber and Demarcus had been trying to reach me, but I'd missed every call and text because my phone was in Darren's car amidst the chaos at the apartment complex.

Demarcus: Mom, Daddy is not having a party for me. Just some cupcakes and some Big K soda at grandma's. He is not even here. I want to come home.

Amber: Did you know my dad was out of prison? He's in Marshall. Too creepy. I'm coming home.

Amber: Demarcus wants to come home tonight, too. Sorry. We're on our way.

And just like that, our private anniversary party became a house full of distraught kids and weary parents.

Chapter 3

We parked and walked into the house. Darren hugged the twins, then the girls went upstairs clinging to one another like two toddlers afraid of getting lost in the mall. Despite their differences and disagreements, the bond between Skylar and Tyler was amazing to behold.

Darren stood next to me in the foyer. He'd read the texts on my phone from Amber and could only sigh right along with me. "I don't even know where to start."

He wasn't alone. Amber had probably been crying, Demarcus was probably upset, and the twins surely needed some wise counsel. We were both heartbroken for all four of our children.

All of a sudden, a scripture popped in my heart from the women's group study of the book of Second Chronicles. I wasn't well versed like Sheila and the other old-school Christians, they seemed to be able to recall scripture at the drop of a hat. Nonetheless, I was thankful for what the Holy Spirit did bring to my remembrance. Maybe the word alone was enough in the moment.

"Babe there's a scripture that says we don't know what to do, but our eyes are on you. I don't know exactly where it is in the Bible, but I know it's there."

Darren nodded. "That's precisely how I feel. Let's pray."

My husband took us before the throne, asking the Lord to give us wisdom and to bring peace into our children's troubled hearts. When we finished the prayer, Darren came up with a plan that shocked me completely. I had thought we'd divide and conquer: I'd talk to Amber and Demarcus while he comforted Tyler and Skylar. But instead he said, "Let's get everyone down here so we can pray together and work through these issues like a family."

I was afraid. Afraid that things might get carried away with emotion, anger, feelings. I didn't want another big dramatic scene at our home. Still, if this was the direction my husband received in prayer, who was I to scoff at it?

Darren got on the intercom and asked everyone to come down, though it wasn't a request so much as a command. Tyler and Skylar sat on the love seat. Demarcus sat between Darren and me on the couch. Amber sat in the chair alone. I gathered Dylan must have been sound asleep.

"First things first," my husband began, "I know it's been a long night for everyone. But we thank God that everyone is here now. Safe in our home. Amber, I'm sorry about the awkward situation in Marshall. It must feel really weird to run into your father after all these years."

"Awkward is an understatement. Mom, did you know he was out?"

"No, baby. I never would have let you to go my small hometown if I'd thought you would run into him."

"What did he say to you?" Skylar wanted to know. "Where did you see him?"

"It was so random. At a gas station. He said hello. He introduced himself as my father, and since he was with a lady who used to work at my elementary school who vouched for him, I knew he was telling the truth. He tried to hug me. He wanted to hold Dylan, which was *not* going to happen. I just...had to get out of there." Amber shook her head.

Tyler surmised. "I don't blame you. Stay away from him. He cray-cray."

"Well, at least your dad wanted to see you," Demarcus spoke in a squeaky voice. "My Daddy wasn't even there. He left me a cupcake and some Big-K soda with a tuna sandwich wrapped in foil. I think the tuna was spoiled 'cause the sticker had yesterday's date on it."

"Oh my gosh! Did you eat it?" I grabbed Demarcus's face and examined his skin and eyes for any sign of illness.

"No. When I opened it, it smelled bad."

"Good," I sighed with relief.

"Come sit with us, Demarcus. We feel your pain." The twins made space for Demarcus and he squished between them.

"At least you didn't almost die in a fire!" Tyler said to him.

"A fire?"

"Yep. That's why we're back. Our momma's place just caught on fire. She was drunk and—"

"Tyler, don't be disrespectful," I cut her off.

She smacked her lips and covered her face, probably trying to avoid rolling her eyes at me, which we had recently established as a no-no.

"But it's true," Skylar cried. "She's a bad mother. Elroy was there earlier. Before the fire. She makes us stay in our room and lock the door when he's there, so nothing will happen. But I'm tired of this. I'm tired of her making bad decisions!"

Demarcus put an arm around Skylar's shoulder. Amber went over and knelt beside the younger kids. "Guys, we're going to be all right. Look at what we have." She pointed toward Darren and me. "We've all got two *good* parents right here. That's all anyone can ask for, right?"

"I was hoping for three," Tyler said.

My husband intervened, "Look, I'm not making excuses for anyone. Being a parent is a very hard job. Not everyone is ready to fulfill that role when they become mothers and fathers. Every child and every parent connected to every child in this room needs prayer. Agreed?"

"Yes. Agreed."

So, again, my husband prayed for the Holley family, asking for forgiveness, understanding, and even more peace.

Now, I know that God is our anchor. Our provider. Our everything. But it sure is nice to be covered in prayer by an earthly husband.

The twins decided to sleep in Amber's room. Demarcus felt left out, so the girls agreed to let him sleep in the room on the grounds that—if Dylan could have spoken—he probably wouldn't have wanted to be the only boy in the room. I nearly laughed at their arrangement. Who would have thought that in a house as big as ours, with all those bedrooms and separate suites, the children would opt to sleep in one room? Sometimes, you just don't need all that space.

Darren and I retired to our bedroom utterly exhausted. All romantic plans were postponed. We fell asleep in each other's arms.

About an hour later, I got up to get some water from the kitchen. I heard laughter coming from Amber's room and almost cried at the miracle. The fact that our children were finding joy in each other's company on a night that was probably one of the most difficult nights of their lives was a testament to the peace that surpasses all understanding. Alongside the bitter events of the evening, the Lord was also planting a harvest of good memories.

Thank You, Lord.

Since we'd had such a horrible night, we all slept in Sunday morning. Or at least we tried to sleep in. The doorbell rang like crazy at around eight-thirty, followed by beating on the door.

"Darren!"

Mother Holley.

"Darren Michael Holley!"

My husband jumped out of bed and answered her on the intercom. "Momma. What are you doing here?"

"Son, quit actin' like you the butler and come open this door."

He took a deep breath and stomped his foot.

I grabbed his robe from the floor and held it up for him.

"Thank you."

Since he'd left the door to our bedroom open and Mother Holley's voice was raised a few octaves, it didn't take much straining to be able to eavesdrop on their conversation below.

"Darren, why did you leave Marcy in jail?"

"She was drunk. She needed to sober up."

"She needed bail money, too!" my mother-in-law added. "I got her out. You owe me seven hundred dollars."

"Momma, that's on you. I can't do nothin' about that."

She challenged him, "Can't or won't?"

"*Won't.* Marcy's got problems. And she's pouring alcohol on top of them. It's only a matter of time before her life catches on fire like her apartment did. I'm just thankful to God my girls weren't hurt."

"Well, they're her girls, too. And have you noticed—Marcy didn't start having all these problems until you got remarried? She was perfectly fine until Angelia came into your life. She was a good mother. A good ex-wife to you. But you just had to go and get married again."

That was my cue to get my robe on and join the conversation. My mother-in-law had every right to her feelings, but I'd be a fool to let her talk bad about me in my own house.

While my husband tried to respectfully disagree, I stuffed my feet into my bunny slippers and shuffled on into the kitchen. "Morning."

"Good morning," Mother Holley chirped as though she hadn't just been calling me a Marcy-wrecker. "I'm so glad you're here, Angelia. There's something else I want to talk to you and Darren about. Well, I really just want to talk to Darren about it. But since I know you gon' have two cents to put in, we might as well all talk about it together."

I gave my husband a *what-does-she-mean?* look. He shook his head slightly.

After pouring a glass of cranberry juice, I sat at the island.

Mother Holley grabbed my glass. "Thank you, sweetheart."

No she didn't! I had heard Darren ask her if she wanted something to drink earlier, but she had declined.

Jesus, take the wheel.

She swallowed hard. "So anyway. Like I was saying. We got a major problem."

"Momma, Marcy is a grown woman. She is *not* my problem."

"Well, you're wrong. So long as she's your girls' mother, she's always gonna be a little bit of your problem," Mother Holley corrected him.

As much as I didn't like what she'd said, there was some truth to her statement. When you have a child with someone, there's always something to deal with regarding that person—

even if it's simply constantly forgiving them for being who they are and forgiving yourself for giving your kid a bad joke for a parent.

"I got something to show you." She pulled two envelopes from her purse. "Attorneys. They're about to take the house. One talking about back taxes. The other one is after the lien for a home improvement loan we took out before your father passed."

Darren took the envelopes and read their contents. The more he read, the more his face wrinkled. "Momma, haven't you paid the taxes these last few years with Dad's life insurance? There was more than enough."

She poked out her lips and shrugged like she was clueless. "Well...you know...I've had other expenses."

"Other expenses like what?"

"Like...curtains. Custom drapes ain't cheap."

Darren started in, "Okay, curtains. What else?"

"You know, other things. Like—"

"Like going to church conventions dressed like Bill Gates's first cousin? Like buying expensive purses? And like going to the boat?"

Mother Holley's mouth popped open.

My husband cut her off before she could even try to deny the final accusation. "Yeah. I know you've been gambling, Momma. I follow Aunt Mabel on Facebook. She posts pictures every time y'all go with the senior center, which is quite often. How much have you lost to the slots?"

She piled her hands on the table and dropped her head on top of the pile. "I lost count, baby. I don't even know. Your momma's not perfect, you know? I just...I miss your father so much. He used to handle everything." Her voice quivered and she sniffed several times. "Your Daddy would put a cap on my spending. Now I don't have anyone to help me."

Darren looked at the letters again. "So. Altogether. How much do you need to keep the house?"

I promise you, this woman took her acting lessons at the same place Tyler took hers because when she raised up to answer, her eyes were still as dry as a bone and her voice was suddenly steady again. "About twenty thousand dollars."

"Uh, that's a no," flew straight up from my spirit and out of my mouth.

Darren and Mother Holley looked at me. Her eyes were laced with anger, his with gratitude, as though he was glad I'd put that big 'no' on the table for us both. Granted, I hadn't meant to blurt out my unbridled thoughts, but I really didn't mind being the bad cop this time.

"We've got three more kids' futures to think about, Mother Holley," I said.

"She's right, Momma."

"What about the Holley legacy? The Holley property, Darren? Your father worked hard to pay off that house. How can you just let it go?"

"That's a very good question. Do you have a good answer?" He asked his mother.

"What do you mean?"

"I mean if it means so much to you, why would you risk it by gambling and blowing through six figures in just three years on *top* of your monthly retirement income?"

Her eye twitched as she probed, "Darren. What about you? Have you spent so much money movin' your wife and her kids into this mini-mansion that you don't even have twenty thousand dollars to spare? Who's the one blowing money now?"

I crossed my arms and pressed my lips together. *Let Darren handle this.*

"Momma, if twenty thousand dollars was all it cost to ensure your well-being, I'd sign the check right now. But if you don't know how to manage money, if you keep trying to keep up with the Joneses and continue to run to the casinos twice a month, twenty grand won't solve the problem."

"Hmph. So you just gonna let your momma live out on the streets while you and your wife livin' in the lap of luxury?"

Darren blinked hard. "I'll always honor you. I always have. But I'm not going to go broke behind it. We'll have to come up with another solution."

Mother Holley snatched the letters from Darren's hands. "I know one thing. If anything happens to me—if I drop dead of a heart attack—it'll be your fault!"

"Don't try to—"

"Nu uh!" she insisted, wagging her finger in my husband's face. "You mark my words. God don't like ugly. He's gonna fix this."

"Mother Holley, we'll be praying that He fixes it for His glory," I said.

"Naw, that ain't what I'm prayin' for. I want Him to fix it another way."

I asked, "What way would be better than a way that brings Him praise and honor?"

She fumed, "*My* way!"

And with that, she let herself out of the house.

I hugged my husband from behind.

"We should have been praying for *my* parent last night, too," he chuckled.

I laughed into his shirt. "Amen and amen."

Chapter 4

Darren left and took Demarcus to go play basketball. I knew he was worried about Mother Holley and needed to clear his mind.

I went into the bathroom and sat on the toilet to have some private prayer time. I needed God to help me understand what was really going on. How in the world did Javar get out of jail? Is Marcus on crack? Is Mother Holley Marcy's new drinking partner?

The more I thought about our issues the angrier I became. I bowed my head in prayer. Lord, please help me through this nightmare; Lord, I don't know what this all means but I know that You see and know all. Lord, help me not to lean to my understanding because right now I have no understanding of this madness. Lord protect my babies through this process. Darren and I are trying our best to be the type of parents You would have us to be but Lord, it's so hard to not wanna cuss or strangle somebody. I know that's not the right thing to do but ain't no sense in me lying to You, because I know You know my heart. I'm trying my best to be a good daughter-in-law too, so please keep me in peace with Mother Holley. Lord, please forgive my thoughts and create in me a clean heart and renew the right spirit within me. I lift my family up to You. In Jesus' name I pray. Amen.

I felt a whole lot better after my prayer. I had been talking to God a lot more than I normally did. Sheila and Sandra Jean told me that forming a prayer life was important. I needed to talk to God every day. Months earlier it was a struggle for me but I found myself talking to God in the car, in the store, while I was cleaning, or even cooking. I was thankful for my new walk with Christ. *I may not be where I should be, but I am proud to say I'm nothing like I used to be.*

I decided to go ahead and take a bath to help calm me some more. I started the water and added my Calgon bath beads. I turned on the jet stream flow, laid back on my bath pillow and closed my eyes. Every muscle in my body began to relax; I felt like I was at a spa. I stayed in the tub for about an hour. I dried off, lotioned up and put my robe on.

I went downstairs to the den to call Amber's grandmother, Peggy and see if she could give me some information on Javar. I hadn't spoken with Peggy in quite some time and had no idea how things would go. When Javar went to prison, I made the decision to just move on with my life. I couldn't keep in contact with his family because they wanted me to "wait for him" like they planned to. It just wasn't going to happen. Aside from a Christmas card here and there for Amber, we didn't have much to do with the Norrells.

Slowly I dialed her number and prepared myself for the call.

After the second ring she answered the phone.

"Praise the Lord, good morning."

"Good morning, Ms. Peggy, it's Angelia. How are you?"

"I'm too blessed to be stressed. How are you? And Amba? And I hear I've got a great-grandson, too!"

"Yes, ma'am. All is well with me. Amber had a son, Dylan. He's so smart and handsome—"

She giggled. "Just like my Javar! You really missed out on my son, Angelia. I knew one day he was gonna be free, bless the name of the Lord!"

Bless her heart, Miss Peggy was still in the last century.

"Is Javar there?"

"No baby, Javar lives over in Necton. Got a trailer house on Daddy's land."

"How long has he been home?"

"Chile, he been here 'bout three or four months. The Lord brought him home. I knew it was just a matter of time before God would do it. He's so good. Thank You Lord, thank You Lord."

I held the phone while Ms. Peggy got her praise on. She loved the Lord and would praise God in the middle of the street if she got the notion. I believe when David wrote I will bless the Lord at all times His praises shall continually be in my mouth, He was talking about Ms. Peggy.

"Ms. Peggy, can you please give me Javar's number? I really need to talk to him about Amber."

"Hold on just a minute; let me get my tablet. You know I writes numbers down."

I laughed because Ms. Peggy reminded me so much of my grandmother. My grandmother had several tablets with phone numbers on them; that's the way they operated in the country.

"Alright, Angie baby; here's the number, (903) 555-5503 and tell Amba that I wanna see my great-granbaby. We folks too, you know!"

"Thanks, Ms. Peggy, and I'll tell Amber what you said."

"Ummm hmm. Alright, God bless you and keep you real good."

"You too," I said and hung up.

Ms. Peggy was a sweetheart. She lived in her own world in her own head with Jesus, but she'd always been good to me and Amber. I would always be Angie and Amber would always be Amba, no matter how many times we tried to correct her. I wondered what name she would give for Dylan. *Probably Dilly,* I thought and laughed.

"Mom, what are you laughing at?" Amber asked, entering the den.

"I just spoke with your grandma Peggy and she still calls you Amba."

"Yeah, she's called me that since I was a little girl."

"Did you talk to my dad?"

"No, not yet. I just got the number and plan to call him in a few minutes."

"Good, because I want to hear what he has to say."

"I don't think that's a good idea."

"Mom, you've got to stop treating me like a little kid. I'll be ok."

"I'm sorry, honey, you'll always be my baby and I just don't want you upset. Why are you up so early anyway?"

"J.D. called me talking stupid, saying that we are going to court. I think he's just mad because I don't really want to talk to him anymore."

"Well honey, unfortunately he's telling the truth. A letter did come stating that you have to go to paternity court."

"When? And why didn't you give it to me?" Amber's face turned red and tears began to form in her eyes.

"I didn't want you to stress out about it. I know you've been up late a lot with Dylan and his head cold, and you've been looking for work. The appointment isn't until next month. There was no need in you worrying about it every day until then. I mean—it is what it is. Why worry until it gets here?"

"You know what, Mom, I don't care. I am so sick of him and his drama. If he wants to go to court then so be it."

I had never seen Amber like this before; she was truly maturing.

"Sweetheart, don't you worry about a thing, you'll get over J.D. and you and Dylan will be ok," I reassured her.

"Get over him? I am through with him forever and I mean it." Amber cried.

I held my baby in my arms and allowed her to release her pain. I hated to see her like this, but I was glad to hear her say she was over J.D. Amber wailed for a while.

"Amber, come on, baby, you've got to get yourself together," I encouraged her.

"I'll be ok. It's like K.J. said, Dylan and I deserve better."

"K.J.?" I said, confused about this new set of initials.

"Yes, Mom. K.J. and I are really good friends. We talk a lot," Amber confessed.

"Whoa, hold on now... you haven't given yourself time to get over J.D.," I warned Amber. Lord knows I didn't want Amber traveling down the road to heartbreak. I knew K.J. was a good kid, but I didn't want Amber rushing into a new relationship.

"Mom, it's not like that. He's genuinely concerned about me and he even said we couldn't go out on a date until I talked to you and Dad."

"How long has this been going on?" I asked, still baffled by it all.

"It's been about three months now." Amber smiled.

"Three months! Why didn't you tell me?"

"Mom, I didn't tell you because I wanted to be sure that we were going somewhere."

"And just where are y'all going?" I quizzed.

"We're not going anywhere. I just wanted to make sure I was interested in dating him seriously before telling you guys."

"I still don't know how I feel about this, Amber. I've got to talk to Darren and see what he says."

"I knew you would say that, K.J. and I will take things slow, it's not like we're trying to get married."

"Wow, sounds like you have this all planned out."

"I really like K.J. and want to date him, so I think it's time for us to move forward."

"I understand what you're saying, but please promise me that you will take things turtle-slow and that you will not have sex with him."

"Mom, I can't believe you said that." Amber looked embarrassed.

"Well there's no need to sugar coat things for you, you're a young adult who knows about sex. I love my grandson, but I don't want another grandbaby until you are married."

"K.J. knows that I plan to be celibate until I get married, and he respects my decision. I told him if he was looking for a good time, he's looking in the wrong direction."

I was so glad to be having this type of conversation with Amber. My mother never talked to me about sex. I remember when I got my cycle, my mother told me to stay away from boys and when I asked why she said, 'Because I said so.' There I was sitting outside on the porch with a pad on, bleeding with no explanation. I wanted to play kickball with all of my friends in the neighborhood.

I remember Billy Edwards asking me to be a team captain and I told him I couldn't and when he asked me why, I told him it was because I was bleeding. I didn't know I wasn't supposed to tell him until Michael Pevito told everybody I was on the rag. Everyone in the neighborhood made fun of me for at least a week. Thank God for Erica and Claudia telling me the real deal.

"Mom, did you hear what I said?" Amber asked, bringing me back to reality.

"Yes baby, I heard you and I'm glad you are making the right decision."

"I'm thankful for Dylan. I learned a lesson from having a baby before marriage. I want a real relationship with my husband, not a one-night stand or a pretend relationship with someone who couldn't care less."

"I'm so proud of you," I said, hugging Amber.

"Ok, now let's call my biological dad. I want to hear what he has to say."

I almost forgot about calling Javar but there was no need for me to stall. Amber was almost grown and could make decisions on her own. I dialed the number and put the phone on speaker so she could hear.

"Hello."

"Hey Javar, it's Angelia," I said nervously.

"Hey Leaha, how you doing?" Javar used the pet name that he'd given me when we first met.

"It's Angelia. I no longer go by that name. Angelia Holley to be exact," I said, putting him in check real quick.

"I can respect that. *Angelia*, how are you doing?"

"All is well with me. When did you get out?"

"I've been out for four months now."

"Four months? Why didn't you call to let me know?" I said furiously.

"Look Angelia, it's by the grace of God that I got out. I really don't want to have this conversation on the phone. Can we meet up somewhere and talk?"

"Meet up for what?"

"I know I've been gone for some years and I've missed out on Amber's life, but I want to do right by her, and by my grandson too," Javar pleaded.

"Speaking of Amber, she's right here with me now."

"Hey, Amber. I know I may have come on a little strong when I saw you last night. I was just excited about seeing you. I want to get to know you and my grandson. I can't change the past, but I can promise you that I will be a father to you and a grandfather to my grandson. I had to get a job and get myself together before approaching you."

"Dad, his name is Dylan Norell." Amber chimed in.

I couldn't believe she was so comfortable calling Javar "Dad" already, especially since it had taken Darren months to earn that name.

"Why doesn't he have his dad's last name?" Javar questioned.

"It's a long story that I don't want to get into right now," Amber said.

"Well, when can I see you and Dylan? I can even come to Lancing Springs so that you won't have to drive down here."

My heart raced as I waited for Amber to respond to Javar's request.

"Well I have your number.Can I think about it and call you with an answer?"

"Yes, take all the time you need. No pressure."

"Ok, Dad, expect a call from me soon."

"Perfect. Thanks for calling and good hearing from you too, Leaha—I mean Angelia."

"Same here."

"Bye, Dad."

Chapter 5

Dylan let out a soft cry through the baby monitor, letting Amber know that he was up. Darren had put baby monitors in every room so we always knew what the baby was up to. Amber left to go check on him and I sat on the couch feeling numb and lost.

I really didn't know how to feel about Javar wanting to be a part of Amber and Dylan's life. I knew Amber was capable of making her own decisions but this was all happening too fast for me. *And did I hear Javar say he was out by the grace of God?* I never heard him mention God before. Maybe he had become a jailhouse minister. Most people I knew who spent time in prison came out either become Muslim or super-Christians for at least a couple of months and then went back to doing the same ole stuff. *Who knows, maybe he is a changed man. Who am I to judge? I'm still trying to learn how to live right myself.*

"Mom, can we talk?" Skylar entered the den interrupting my thoughts.

"Sure honey, what's on your mind?"

"I don't ever want to go back to my mom's house, and I don't want Dad to make me," Skylar said, looking bewildered.

"I can't say what will happen, Skylar, but I can tell you Darren will make sure that whatever happens will be what's best for everyone involved."

"What's best for who? What y'all talking about?" Tyler asked, walking into the den and plopping down on the couch.

"I was saying that I don't want to ever go back to Mom's house."

41

I held my breath waiting on Tyler's reply, because she normally defended Marcy.

"You know what, sis? You right. She straight trippin' and she lettin' a dude make her look real dumb right about now."

I was surprised by Tyler's response and silently agreed with her, but I needed to let her know what she said was out of order. "Tyler, I know you have strong feelings about what has taken place, but Marcy is still your mother so let's not call her dumb."

"Ok then, what would you call it?" Tyler asked, putting me on the spot.

"I would say that we all make mistakes and sometimes those mistakes hurt those that we love, but the good news is that we can ask for forgiveness. We can ask for forgiveness for those that we hurt and try to work through those issues. God is faithful and if He brings us to it, He will bring us through it."

"Alrighty then, Oprah Winfrey." Tyler laughed. "Seriously though, how many times do we have to keep going through drama with her? She too old to keep doing this."

"Tyler, I understand your frustration and I agree that it's a lot to deal with, but nothing is too hard for God to work out."

"Mom, you're right. We need to pray and ask God to help us deal with our issues. I don't like the way this has me feeling. I couldn't sleep last night," Skylar confessed.

"I slept good than a mug, I didn't have to worry about a roach crawling on me or being too hot," Tyler said.

Tyler is just too real for me. I was glad that God had worded my mouth because I didn't want to say the wrong thing to the girls.

"The good news is that you're safe and now we can move forward and we'll see what happens in the days to come."

"I agree. Miss Earlene said as believers we may go through some things but we won't stay there," Skylar reminded us.

Ever since her accident, Skylar had crazy faith and tried to look at the bright side of any given situation.

Amber returned, carrying Dylan in her arms. "Mom, can we get out of the house today and go to Elk Manor and do some shopping?"

"Hey, Mimi's little guy. Give Mimi a kiss," I cooed and Dylan formed his lips to kiss me. Moments like those, I couldn't imagine my life without him.

"I think that's good idea, 'cause I need some more kicks... I mean shoes," Tyler pointed out because she knew I had no idea what kicks were.

"Ok girls, let's get dressed. I could use some retail therapy right now."

I was glad to be having some time alone with the girls. I rushed upstairs and found some clothes to put on. I decided to put on a black and silver bling t-shirt with the words "God First" on it and a pair of black jeans. I found my pair of silver and bling cross earrings and finished up my look with my black cap with the blinged-out cross on it that I bought at Beauty Discount Center. I decided not to get fully made up, so I glossed my lips and put on some eyeliner.

I went downstairs and the girls were all sitting on the couch. I was shocked to see them all in jeans and red shirts that read "Thing 1," "Thing 2," and "Thing 3."

"Ok can someone explain to me what the shirts mean?" I asked.

"It means we are sisters: Amber is "Thing 1" because she's the oldest and I let Skylar be "Thing 2" since we are twins and of course you have to save the best for last so I'm "Thing 3.""

"Oh ok, I get it."

"Yeah, it was Tyler's idea," Amber stated. "I bought them a few weeks ago. I was going to wait for a special occasion, but given this crazy weekend, I think it's special enough that we all survived it."

I stood there for a moment just staring at the three of them in awe. Seeing Tyler wanting to have a sisterly bond is such a blessing.She's come a long way.

"What's wrong, Ms. Angelia? You don't like them?" Tyler frowned.

"No sweetheart, I love it. As a matter of fact, let me take a picture of you guys; I want to put it on my Facebook page." I grabbed my phone to take the picture.

"One day you'll upgrade and go to Instagram with the rest of the world." Tyler laughed.

"Whatever… I'm good with my Facebook page, I don't have time for all that other stuff. Alright, y'all. Smile!"

I took three different poses of the girls and immediately uploaded the photos to my page. I tagged Darren in the post. "Let's rock and roll."

We went to the garage and got in the truck. Amber sat up front with me while Dylan sat in the back seat in between the twins. I put on my Tasha Page Lockhart CD and headed to Elk Manor. Midway through the trip Amber's phone rang and startled all of us because of her weird ring tone. The phone was singing "Your boo is calling. Your boo is calling."

Both of the girls giggled and said in unison, "It's K.J."

They know about K.J. already?

Tyler and Skylar were chatting and making kissing noises while I tried to eavesdrop.

Amber ended the call before I could find out what she was saying.

"That was K.J. He was just checking on me and Dylan."

"Awwwwwww, how sweet," Skylar sang.

"Girl, quit playing. You know K.J. want you to be his girl for real," Tyler added.

Amber didn't reply, she just smiled.

We arrived at the mall and headed to my favorite store, Macy's.

Macy's was having a 40% off sale and I was ecstatic. After being in Macy's for almost an hour I found four dresses and headed to the dressing room to try them on. Tyler and Skylar decided to head to Rue 21 and Lady Footlocker to see if they could find anything of interest. Amber and Dylan stayed with me.

"Ok what do you think of this one, Amber?" I asked, doing a runway spin as I tried on the last dress.

"I think it looks great, just like the others."

Dylan started squirming and whining in his stroller.

"Let me get dressed so we can find a place to change and feed Dylan. He's probably getting tired."

"Yeah, he's ready to break free."

I hurriedly changed my clothes and went to the register to pay for my purchases. Luckily I was able to go to the register of an employee who had just opened her line.

Amber took Dylan to the restroom to change him. I stayed behind and watched the stroller and our bags. I made sure she took her changing pad and sanitizer with her. I despised public bathrooms.

I pulled out my cell phone to see if I had any missed calls from Darren. I didn't have any so I guessed he and Demarcus were having a good time.

"Alright he's all changed. Let's go to the food court and get some of those delicious cookies."

"Sounds good, we'll pass both of the stores the girls planned to go to so they can join us too."

Amber and I walked toward the food court as Skylar and Tyler were coming out of Rue 21.

"Perfect timing. We're about to get some cookies," I said.

"I love the chocolate chip cookies," Skylar said, licking her lips.

"Ms. Angelia, ain't that your cousin, Claudia over there?" Tyler said, pointing.

I looked up and saw Claudia. She was with a guy, but I could only see the back of his head.

"That sure is Claudia," Amber confirmed.

We walked in the direction of Claudia to catch up with her before she got away.

"Claudia... Claudia," I said, calling her name to get her attention.

Claudia and her companion turned around and to my surprise her companion was none other than Sherman Johnson.

All of the blood drained from my body; all I could see was red. I tried my best not to let the children know that I was livid.

"Angelia, what are you doing in Elk Manor?" Claudia asked nervously.

"The question is what are *you* doing in Elk Manor?" I said, choosing my words carefully.

"Yo Claudia, this yo new man? Dang, he fine. For real, he look better than old boy you brought to the BBQ," Tyler stated.

"Angelia, it's good to see you. Are these your children?" Sherman asked calmly, as if I didn't just catch him with my cousin.

"Yes, these are my girls and my grandson," I said, glaring at him.

"Oh, I remember when Claudia told me about his dedication," Sherman pointed out.

"Oh is that right?" I said sarcastically.

So that means Claudia has been seeing Sherman for quite a while now. How dare she go behind my back to date my ex who, by the way, is an ex because she convinced me to break up with him. I wonder if Erica knows about this. All kinds of questions were running through my mind.

"We're headed to the movies. Come on, Claudia, we don't want to be late," Sherman said.

"Oh ok… yeah, we better get moving. Angelia, I'll call you later," Claudia stuttered.

"Yeah, you do that," I said, breathing heavily.

Chapter 6

Unbelievable, I can't believe Claudia has been seeing Sherman. I need to get out of this mall before I explode. Claudia told me a few months ago she was practicing celibacy and was waiting on Mr. Right. Wait just a minute. Does she think Sherman is Mr. Right? Oh no no no, if she thinks I'm going to let her have Sherman, she got another think coming.

"Ms. Angelia, you alright? You don't look too good," Tyler said.

"Oh I'm perfectly fine. Just need to get some air. I'm a little tired," I lied.

"Mom, did you know Claudia was dating someone?" Amber asked.

"No, I had no idea," I managed to say.

"That explains why she wasn't home last night when I was in Marshall."

Ok now this is too much. Claudia wasn't home, which means she was with Sherman, spending the night with Sherman, doing God knows what! I felt little beads of sweat forming on my forehead.

"Let's get Mom some water and something in her stomach," Skylar said with concern.

"Guys, I'm great. Never better," I said, trying to convince myself. "Let me sit down while you go get the food. Amber, you can leave Dylan here with me."

"Are you sure?" They all asked in unison.

"Yes, now go… scat, get me a slice of pizza and a Sprite."

The children left to go get the food and I pulled out my phone to call Erica.

I was glad she was on speed dial. My hand was shaking so there's no way I could have dialed her number.

Erica picked up on the first ring.

"Hey Angelia, what's going on, girl?"

"That's what I was calling to ask you."

"Oh, you found out. Girl, your ex lookin' good. He got a new truck, working in the oil field, got a nice, brick trailer house, and I heard he joined church last Sunday," Erica said, as if she was proud.

"Erica... what? Wait... slow down; who are you talking about?"

"Javar... duh. Who else would I be talking about?" Erica smacked her lips.

"I was calling to ask you about Claudia dating Sherman."

"Oh. Pshhh. Girl yeah, she been dating him for a minute. She ran into him when she went to Elk Manor for a job interview. She got hired and she's moving there next weekend."

"What job? Better yet... why Sherman?"

"What you mean 'why Sherman?' Angelia, girl you a trip. You got a man; why you worried about who Sherman date?"

"Newsflash... I used to date him; we were practically engaged." I raised my voice, almost forgetting I was in the mall.

"Key word *used* to, Angelia. Why you sweating him when you got 'Mr. All That' Darren?" Erica said rudely.

"What's that supposed to mean?" I was really irritated with her tone.

"It means that you've always been such a goody-goody and you seem to think you're the only person who deserves happiness. It means that you've always thought you were better than us even though it was our mother who took you in.

"So what if Claudia is going out with Sherman. That's her business. It has nothing to do with you. What you and Sherman had must not have been too precious to him because if it was he wouldn't have asked Claudia out."

I hung up the phone because I was flabbergasted by Erica's words. Defending Claudia was one thing, but for her to say all of those horrible things was just disheartening. I looked up to them as if they were my big sisters. Throughout our adult years we didn't get to see one another as much but we communicated. I included them in my life. I made sure Amber and Demarcus were a part of their lives. My moving to Lancing Springs didn't mean that I thought I was better; we moved because of Darren's job. Why should I have to be ridiculed for that? I always knew there was a little jealousy, but I thought we had grown past that. *Guess that's what I get for thinking.*

I got Dylan out of his stroller and held him close to my heart and I felt tears welling up in my eyes. I sniffled and got a Kleenex out of my purse to dab my eyes. I couldn't allow the children to see me like this.

"Mom, we got you a sausage pizza since you didn't really say what kind you wanted," Skylar said, setting the pizza on the table.

"That will work. Thanks, sweetheart."

"You sure you ok, Ms. Angelia?"

"I'm fine and once I finish eating I'll be even better. Did you see anything you wanted in any of the stores today?" I asked, changing the subject.

"I wanna go to Lady Foot Locker and get a pair of the new Nike Air Max but they're $200.00, and if I get them I promise I won't ask for anything else for at least 2 months," Tyler stated, acting like a contestant on Let's Make A Deal.

"A whole two months, Tyler? Yeah right," Skylar teased.

"Girl, I'm serious… I need those kicks in my life," Tyler said in between chews.

"Shoes that cost that much must have glitter and gold on them," Amber added, laughing.

"Tyler, that is a little steep but I guess you can get the shoes. You've got to take really good care of them, though." I knew Darren would question me about the shoes later, but at the moment, I didn't have the energy to listen to Tyler re-state her case a thousand ways.

"I will, I won't even let them get dirty," she pleaded.

"Did you see anything you wanted, Skylar?"

"I saw a couple of dresses I want in Rue 21 and I have a coupon so can we stop there, too?"

"I want to go to Ross when we get back home to pick up a few things and I also want to get a job application," Amber said.

"Ok, let's finish eating," I said.

We finished eating and went to Footlocker and Rue 21. I still couldn't get my conversation with Erica off of my mind. I was going to have to pray about this thing and have the ladies in my prayer group pray with me as well. I was really feeling a spirit of heaviness in my heart.

When we arrived at the car I passed Amber the keys and buckled myself into the passenger's seat. I put my shades on and sat quietly and meditated on Psalm119:28. *My soul melts from heaviness; Strengthen me according to your word.*

I must have dozed off for a few minutes because I heard Amber calling me. "Mom, are you getting out or staying in?"

"I'll stay in since it looks like Dylan is sleep, poor baby. He's probably worn out. Here's my credit card. Go ahead and get you a few items, don't take too long."

"Ok, come on, Skylar and Tyler. Y'all come on help me. That'll speed up the time."

The girls went into Ross while I stayed with Dylan. I decided that I couldn't wait until Wednesday night to deal with my issues. I called Sheila.

"Hey girlfriend, how you doing?" Sheila asked.

"Not too good. I saw my cousin, Claudia with my ex-boyfriend, Sherman today," I said, getting straight to the point.

"Ok and what happened?" Sheila quizzed me.

"Nothing happened. I saw them *together* as a *couple* and they both acted as if it was *no big deal*."

"Why should it be a big deal?"

"Sheila, for God's sake; he's my *ex!*" I explained. "We were in love! We were intimate! We made promises to one another. I mean, we didn't actually follow through, but…it just doesn't seem right for him to be with my cousin of all people. It's like my whole heart just melted when I saw them together."

"Ok and you're married now, Angelia. It sounds to me like you are still harboring feelings for Sherman. That's what's we call a soul tie."

"Soul tie? What's that?"

"A soul tie is like a linkage in the soul realm between two people. It can be very dangerous. Even twenty years down the road, a person may still think of their first lover, even if they are across the country and happily married with a family."

"How do you get rid of this so-called tie *if* you have one?" I asked, not wanting to admit that I was guilty. Truth be told: A little part of me always wondered what might have been

52

between Sherman and me. He would always be the one that got away.

"Angelia, you've got to pray and ask God to help you get rid of it. You have to take back any words of affirmation that you've vowed—things like, '*I will love you forever,*' or '*I could never love another man.*' Those words need to be renounced. They are spoken commitments that need to be undone verbally. As Proverbs 21:23 tells us, "Whoso keepeth his mouth and his tongue keepeth his soul from troubles. The tongue has the ability to bring the soul great troubles and bondage."

"I made those vows to Sherman, but I was young back then and didn't know any better." I felt ashamed.

"That may be true, but that's why you're so upset with him for being with Claudia. Your soul remembers what your mind forgot. Been there done that."

"Wait a minute… not *you,*" I said, surprised.

"Girl, I told you I'm not perfect. We all struggle with something. Also, you need to get rid of any old pictures, gifts, rings anything that connects you with Sherman."

"This is serious stuff. I've never heard any of this before."

"I didn't know about it myself until we had a women's conference some years ago."

"Alright, Sheila, I've got to go. The children are coming back to the car."

"Girlfriend, hang in there. Repent to God about the soul tie and ask Him to take it away from you. You need to renounce the tie. I'll be praying for you as well."

"Thanks, Sheila, talk to you soon."

"Have a blessed evening."

53

My head was spinning like crazy. I was dealing with too much: Javar coming home, Marcus disappointing Demarcus on his birthday, Marcy and the fire, Mother Holley, Claudia dating Sherman, and now Sheila telling me I have a soul tie. Enough is enough.

Chapter 7

When I got off the phone with Sheila, I took a minute to evaluate what she was saying—trying to make logical sense of it. I had to admit to myself I wasn't completely sold on Sheila's advice. All of this soul-tie stuff sounded too weird and spooky, like some kind of crazy voodoo. People like Sheila and Miss Earlene could be too deep at times. When they started talking about things like "spiritual warfare" and "the enemy," sometimes I tuned out because…well…I really wasn't trying to hear all that. If I could just be forgiven of my sins and live a happy, blessed life, that was all I cared to know.

Even after Tyler had blabbed at the dinner table that Claudia had a fine new boyfriend and my face turned sour, I still didn't believe I needed to break any spiritual ties.

Darren caught the change in my expression, but he didn't say anything at that moment. He'd waited until later, when we were getting dressed for bed.

"So…who's Claudia's new boyfriend?"

"Huh?" I continued wrapping my hair as though his words hadn't pushed the panic button within me.

"The guy your cousin is seeing. You looked like you could slap somebody when Tyler mentioned him. What's his name—Sherman?"

I tried to keep my breathing steady as I applied Vaseline to my lips and under my eyes. "He's, you know, a guy from back home."

"You know him?"

"Everybody knows everybody in Marshall." I chuckled nervously.

Darren stood behind my chair and looked at me via my vanity mirror. "Did you *know* him know him?"

I shrugged casually. "He's an ex."

My husband squinted. "Why do you care so much that he's seeing Claudia?"

"I don't care about *him* seeing Claudia, I care about *her* seeing him. She's my cousin. Cousins don't date cousins' exes. It's in the rule book."

"I'm sure in a small town, people swap exes all the time. It's not like she had a boatload of men to choose from."

"Yes. She did. There's got to be at least three million eligible black men in the United States of America. Why she chose *my* ex is beyond me."

"I think you need to get over it. All's well that ends well," he said. "Don't let this dude—or whatever—come between you and Claudia. From what I can tell, she and Erica are the only people from your family who have been there for you through thick and thin."

At some level, I knew my husband was right. But I wasn't ready to admit that he was onto something just yet. So I put off the soul-tie-breaking shenanigans for another week, thinking that maybe when I started being super-holy, I'd do serious spiritual stuff like renouncing and talking to the devil and breaking magic spells.

In the meantime, there was real life to deal with, starting with Javar and Amber. He was dead-set on seeing Amber and Dylan again and being a part of their lives. He had also apparently added me to his daily text list because every morning around nine, he sent some kind of picture with a scripture or an affirmation on it.

Really? I guess he calls himself a text-evangelist these days.

If it wasn't Javar bugging me with encouragement, it was Mother Holley sending messages through the twins. She'd stopped talking to Darren since I shut down her request for 20k. Yet, she still needed him from time to time. Since she could no longer afford for someone to maintain her lawn, Mother Holley had sent word through Tyler for my husband to come over and cut the grass.

Darren went over with K.J. and a few more players and took care of the lawn, but he told me that she stayed inside the house the whole time, looking out her window like somebody crazy. Of course, he didn't say the "crazy" part—that's just how I pictured it.

The regular school year had begun and already the twins and Demarcus were on restrictions for having C's on their progress reports. I hoped they would get their grades up the actual grading period ended. I didn't feel like grounding all three of them. That would be torture on me because—surprise! surprise!—Darren would be too busy with football season to help enforce anything.

Honestly, I was tired of complaining about my life in my own head. Things just got so overwhelming, though, like all I ever did was put out fires.

And speaking of fires, Marcy was still going in and out of drunken spells. She'd call our house at 11:30 p.m. fussing about one thing or another, her words slurring from the alcohol. I decided it best to block her number on the house phone. That was the least I could do to protect myself from her influence. I was sure she still called the girls, but I think they were getting tired of hearing their mother in that condition. They deserved better.

When my mother passed away, of course I was heartbroken and devastated. But I was glad that at least I could say my mother didn't finish raising me because she couldn't, not because she wouldn't.

I knew girls whose mothers had abandoned them, left them to be raised by their grandmothers because momma wanted to get her I'm-still-young-and-fly on. Or maybe they were addicted to something or some man. Either way, not having a mom available for whatever reason can send a girl off into dozens of unloving relationships. I knew that for a fact already, so I certainly didn't want such foolishness for the twins.

My own foolishness with Marcus was still haunting me. While pounding away on the treadmill one weekday morning, his named flashed on my phone's screen.

I moved the dial left and slowed the pace to 3.0 miles an hour. "Hello?"

"Good morning," he chirped.

"Good morning."

"Sounds like you're out of breath. I didn't interrupt—"

"I'm on the treadmill." I cut him off before he could say something vulgar.

"Oh. I was about to say—if you can stop to answer the phone, things must not be going well in the bedroom."

Lord God, I can't stand him. Can You send him away? "Do you have any idea how vile and inappropriate you are right now?"

Demarcus laughed. "Is that all you have to say? No cussing? No yelling?"

"Is that what you want from me? You want me to get all excited and act a fool over you? Not gonna happen again, Marcus. I'm through with you. Period. In fact, this is our last phone conversation. I won't be accepting any more calls from you. Only text messages and snail mail. So say what you want to say right now 'cause this is it, good buddy."

"How can we raise a child without talking?"

"Just act like we've both got laryngitis. Forever."

He laughed again. "Girl, you so crazy! That's why I still love you. And my son."

"Well, I'm glad you got it out of your system. I'm going to hang up the phone now."

"Wait! I wanted to talk to you about Demarcus's birthday party."

"The party that *didn't happen*?" I asked.

"Yes. I mean, no. It didn't happen *that* weekend. But you know my birthday is coming up. I was thinking I could do a double-party. For me and him. To make it up. I'm gonna call it The Two-Marcus Turn-up. Got some flyers made and everything."

"Umm...that's gonna be a no." I slid the speed back up to 4.0 because this conversation was dragging my heart rate too low.

"But—"

"No buts, Marcus. You already disappointed him once. Why would I set him up for you to do it again?"

"I'm his father! I have a right to see him!"

"You have an obligation to support him, too, in more ways than one."

"You want to take this to court?" he threatened.

59

"Sitting in a court of law with attorneys and a judge to discuss your history with Demarcus would be my pleasure," I countered. "Just be sure to bring your check stubs to the meeting."

"*This* is why people call y'all *baby mommas*!" he yelled.

My only regret about that conversation was that I didn't get to hang up before he did.

When the phone rang seconds later, I answered in a huff, "What?!"

"Umm...hello? Is this Angelia?" a sweet sound tone through.

"Oh, I'm sorry, Miss Earlene. I thought you were someone else."

"I see. Well, I was callin' 'cause I wanted you to come get the stuff I got for Dylan."

"You are going to spoil this child rotten!"

"Naw, honey, I don't think I could ever beat you and Darren doing that."

"You're right about, Miss Earlene. I'll be over in just a second."

I finished the last mile on my treadmill and then rushed over to Miss Earlene's with the blood still pumping in my veins. The elevated rate was also due to the conversation with Marcus, which didn't sit well in my gut. *I so need to be through with him.*

I rang Miss Earlene's doorbell and she came to the door without a bag in hand, which irritated me somewhat. Don't get me wrong—I like Miss Earlene and all, but sometimes she just wants me to "sit a spell" when all I really want to do is get back to my house and try to catch up on life, as if that will ever really happen.

When she came to the door, I tried to give myself an easy out. "Hi, Miss Earlene. Sorry I can't stay long. I just finished exercising. Need to get in the shower."

She held open the glass door and motioned for me to come inside. "Oh, chile, a little sweat ain't never hurt nobody. Come on in and sit a spell."

I knew it. "No, I can't. I'm behind on housework as it is."

"In that case, I won't take long." She opened the door wider.

My good southern upbringing kicked in. I followed her down the main corridor to her back patio. No baby gift bag in sight. We sat on her wicker furniture.

"Miss Earlene—"

"Angelia, I won't hold you long, honey, I just got to help you with something."

My eyes widened. "Me?"

"Yes. You. When I talked to you earlier and you answered the phone with a snap in your voice—"

"I'm sorry, Miss Earlene. I didn't look at the screen first. I had just gotten off the phone with my second husband, and he had just gotten on my last nerve."

"Okay. So I got to tell you something. And I don't want to you to think bad of me or nobody else."

"Um...okaaay."

"Sheila asked me to pray for you. She didn't say what for, exactly, but that you needed to be released from your past so you can enjoy your present."

"She did, huh?" Couldn't help but feel some kind of way about Sheila sharing my business. *Church folk sure can gossip.*

"She didn't give me no details, so you don't need to get offended. This is what sisters do for one another—we pray.

And then, when necessary, the Lord give us a unction about what to say to one another. It just be a confirmation of what He done already told the other person anyway."

My lips remained still.

"Now, I know you didn't ask for my advice. But given what you just told me and what the Lord already dropped in my spirit, I'd say you need to get rid of your feelings—good, bad, and indifferent—toward all your exes if you plan on living in peace and harmony with Mr. Holley. You got to release 'em."

The hair on my arms stood at attention because this was indeed only a confirmation of the very thoughts that seemed to be invading my common sense when I sat quietly with the Lord. At that point, I didn't see a need to try to keep Miss Earlene in the dark any longer. I told her everything I'd told Sheila about Sherman, plus I told her about Marcus. "I don't know why it seems like they both still have a place in my heart."

"It seems like it 'cause it is so. But you can be free from it, free to give your whole self first to the Lord and then to your husband."

"That's what I want. To be free."

"Then speak it. Say 'it's over'."

"It's over," I spoke into the atmosphere. "I break the soul-tie with Marcus Jackson, Sherman Johnson, Javar Norell, and anyone else who's still got a piece of my heart and soul, in Jesus' name!"

After hearing those words spoken from the depths of my heart, released through my trembling lips, the next breath I breathed in felt like a giant whoosh of fresh air in my soul.

"Thank you, Lord!" I cried out.

"Glory to God!" Miss Earlene echoed as we praised Him for freedom.

That morning, I was a soul-tie-machete by the power of Christ in me.

And I felt cleaner, freer than I had in a long, long time. I wasn't sure which demons or spirits or angels heard me. I just know something happened.

Chapter 8

I'd gone goo-goo-ga-ga over my grandson altogether. Dylan was the most perfect baby—really! He only cried when he was wet, hungry, or if certain strangers tried to hold him. No one knew Dylan's hidden criteria. He liked whom he liked and cried otherwise.

Dylan was getting to that stage where he could communicate more with grunts and sounds, and he loved to play patty-cake. I could already tell he was going to be a genius.

Since he'd started scooting, Amber and I had to baby-proof the house. We spent one Saturday morning stopping up all the electrical outlets and rigging the cabinets so Dylan couldn't open them. He had outgrown the basinet. It was time for a real baby bed, which almost sent Amber into a meltdown. "Mom, I can't believe he's growing up so fast. My baby is turning into a toddler already."

"Before you know it, he'll be walking. And talking. And in pre-school—"

"Okay, okay." She put the last outlet cover in place in the living room. "I get the picture."

I helped her off the floor and gave her a hug. "Don't worry. He'll always be your baby, just like you'll always be mine."

Amber hugged me tightly and didn't let go when I released. I squeezed her frame and asked, "What's wrong?"

"Mom. Dylan—"

"What's wrong with Dylan?" Fear shot through my veins.

"Nothing. Except he doesn't have a dad."

"He does have a father figure. Darren loves him. Demarcus is crazy about him. He'll have plenty of males around to help him become a wonderful young man."

"But it's not the same as your *real* parent." Amber pushed away from me. "I really want him to know J.D. But I don't think JD will have any part in his life if I push for child support. I've been watching what's happening between Demarcus and Mr. Marcus. I don't want that for Dylan."

"But whether or not J.D. steps up to the plate isn't your choice to make. It's *his* choice," I told her.

I wished I could have called Darren in for back-up, but as usual, he was gone on a Saturday morning, handling football business.

To my dismay, Amber seemed to have thought ahead of me. "But he's hardly ever here. And I don't want Demarcus to feel like he *has* to be a father to Dylan. I want him to have a childhood, you know?"

Her words stung as they inadvertently reminded me that I'd robbed her of a carefree childhood.

"So what are you going to do, Amber? The court date is Tuesday."

"So... J.D. is coming over here tomorrow. We'll go get something to eat. So we can talk. About Dylan."

"J.D. all by himself or J.D. and *Nicole*?"

"He's not with Nicole anymore," Amber quickly informed me with the slight hint of a smile.

Lord, Jesus, help us today. "How do you know he's not with her anymore?"

"Because he told me."

"Has he ever lied to you before?"

"Well...yeah, but—"

"Then how do you know he's not lying now?"

Amber tore away from my reach and headed toward the steps. "I need you to stop being so negative, Mom. People can change, you know."

Ain't that much changin' in the world without Jesus.

I watched, speechless, as she stomped up the staircase. I knew that attitude—the one where you already know everything and it's going to take a huge letdown before you actually realize that someone is playing you despite all the warnings.

Lord, don't let her fall too hard.

When J.D. showed up Sunday—an hour after the agreed upon time, mind you—Darren and I did our best to receive him in our home without being ugly.

"Hello, J.D. How's your mother?" was the most sincere greeting I could produce.

"She cool."

My husband forced a normal handshake from the boy. "Good to see you, J.D."

"For real," he replied. "Where's Amber?"

"She'll be down in a second. Would you like to come inside?" I invited.

"Naaaa. I'll wait in the car."

My husband opened the door wider. "You'll wait inside."

J.D.'s nostrils flared, but his body complied.

My body temperature was already up by five degrees, and yet I led him to my white couch. "I've got some pictures for your mom." He sat next to my husband and I while I sorted through the 4x6 prints.

"You mean those Amber put on Facebook? "

"Yes. They're just something to document his growth. We'll hire a photographer and set up shoot here at the house when he turns one," I said, handing him four pictures.

"I hope so 'cause those on Facebook got my son lookin' like a nerd," J.D. laughed. He held up my favorite picture—the one with Dylan in one of his church suits. "Who put that bowtie on him?"

I answered, "I did."

J.D. straightened his face. "My bad. I'm just sayin'. Dylan ain't gon' be no pretty, book-smart boy. He needs some knowledge from the streets, you know what I'm sayin'? I can't wait to get him his first tat."

This boy right here is cuckoo.

Amber hopped down each stair on her tiptoes, her face glowing with anticipation. "Hey J.D.," she said, approaching him.

We all stood.

"Hey. You look good, girl. What's all this?" He ran his fingers through her straightened, ombre-dyed hair.

"New color."

He bobbed his head up and down. "I like."

"Thank you."

Next came Tyler and Skylar toting Dylan and his baby bag, respectively. Tyler dropped Dylan in J.D.'s arms, and Skylar hung the bag's strap on Amber's shoulder.

Of course, Dylan became fussy, being abruptly transferred into the arms of someone he barely knew. J.D. tried to bounce him up and down. "Don't worry, dude. It's me. Your dad."

Amber tried to take him.

"No, honey," I interrupted, "he needs to get to know his father. Right?"

J.D.'s eyes flashed with fear. "Yeah, but not right now. I'll see him when we get back."

"Oh, he's going to dinner with you two," I gladly informed him.

"I'm just sayin', you know, how can we talk with him crying?"

I laughed sarcastically. "It's hard living life with a baby, right? I'm just sayin'."

Darren tugged my shirt, letting me know I'd said enough.

"We'll see you back in a little while," my husband said as he escorted them to the door with my grandson still whimpering.

Cry, Baby Dylan! Cry to your heart's content!

With Amber and the baby out of the house, Darren and I planned some quality time with the other kids. Since our stay at Big Wolf Lodge, they were always chomping at the bit to do some kind of activity together. Tyler and Demarcus were super-competitive, not to mention my husband. Skylar and I just looked on and teased them.

That night, we decided we'd do miniature golf and race cars at a nearby mom-and-pop entertainment center. Both games were every-man-for-himself, so we were all enthralled by the 5th hole when I got a text from Amber stating what I already knew: *J.D. is a LIAR and a JERK! He doesn't DESERVE to be Dylan's father!!!*

I didn't say anything to Darren about it. Just kept on playing like I had before. I took her message as confirmation that God had finally taken the scales off my daughter's eyes so she could see who and what she was dealing with. I know it had to hurt, but sometimes, that's how the truth goes, and Amber needed to come to that conclusion once and for all for herself.

When we got back from the entertainment center, the girls kidnapped Dylan from Amber's room while I went in to speak with her. She vented for the next half-hour about how J.D. had only come to see her because he wanted her to sign papers, basically withdrawing her request for child support. Now that the D-N-A results had proven he was the father, she suppose he thought this was his next opportunity to escape his financial responsibilities.

When Amber refused to sign the papers, he had gotten angry. "Mom, he was so...evil. He even called me the n-word."

"Oh, wow." Somehow, all the other things he'd said didn't hit me quite like that one.

"I know. He's just...stupid."

"I know, honey, but he'll always be Dylan's father." I swallowed hard and tried to remember the words Miss Earlene had spoken to me. "The best thing you can do is forgive him and release him in your heart. It's called breaking a soul tie. And the sooner you break the ungodly alliances you've made with him, the better."

Amber leaned over onto my shoulder and cried her eyes out. "Mom, I just can't believe I was *this wrong* about him. Why did God let this happen?"

"I don't know, but I do know that Jesus came to restore the peace the enemy tricks us out of. It's been that way since the Garden of Eden, honey, don't get too down on yourself."

She wiped her eyes roughly. "Let's do it."

"Do what?"

"Break the soul tie."

"Alrighty then." I got down on my knees.

Amber followed suit.

And then I led my daughter in prayer as she repeated after me, renouncing the stronghold of the relationship with J.D. and asking the Lord for guidance as a mother to my grandson.

After we said, "Amen," Amber looked at me and asked, "Is that it?"

"Yep."

"Just words?"

"Words spoken in faith are more powerful than you know."

Chapter 9

Isaiah 26:3 was quickly becoming my breakfast, lunch, and dinner. *Thou wilt keep him in perfect peace, whose mind is stayed on thee: because he trusteth in thee.* Without that scripture, I would have fallen back into the same funk I did the previous year during football season. The more I prayed and thought about my situation, the more I realized that my third marriage would never be perfect. Darren was a very competitive man. He enjoyed coaching football, he was disciplined, and he was very dedicated to his job. I could either pout about it for five months out of the year or I could lean extra hard on the Lord while supporting my husband all the more during those football months.

Besides, he worked hard, long hours from August to December—the last thing he needed was to come home to a bitter wife. Even if I did think he was wrong for being "married" to football, me having an attitude the whole time wasn't going to fix anything. Only the Lord could change his heart. In the meantime, it looked like He was changing *my* heart instead.

Apparently there was something to all this scripture meditation my Bible study group talked about all the time.

I had to admit, though, that Friday night football games were quite an outing. The twins, Amber, Demarcus, and I had gotten into our routine. We even had custom portable stadium chairs with our names embroidered on the back. I figured if I couldn't beat the football hoopla, I might as well join it.

Even Dylan enjoyed the screaming and hollering. He clapped like he knew exactly what was going on every time we scored a touchdown. And he mimicked the crowd's "oohs" and "aahs", which gave everyone surrounding us quite a laugh. My ▮▮▮▮▮▮was a ham already.

One particular Friday night, the game went down to the wire. We were tied 21-21 with Luketon High School with only four minutes and twenty-three seconds left. My husband was fussing at the offense so bad, I felt sorry for the boys. "Y'all are playin' like this is Pop Warner! I could get my nine-year-old son, Demarcus out here; he'd do a better job! Tell you what, we'll come back out here after it's over and have practice 'cause I'm sure none of you has broken a sweat since the first quarter! Y'all better get your head in the game or we've got a long night ahead of us!"

"Oh no. Come on, K.J.," I heard Amber moan under her breath.

I dipped my chin and glared at her. "K.J., huh?"

She tried to blush. "Yes. He and I were talking about going to get a burger or something after the game. If they lose, he won't be free to leave."

Seeing as I was married to the coach, I felt her pain. "Honey, K.J.'s a really good player. School and football are first in his life right now."

"Mom, we're just friends," she whined with annoyance.

Tyler whipped herself around and butted into our conversation. "But K.J. is fine, though, Miss Angelia. And you're right—he's good. Amber got to get him before the groupies do 'cause he's about to blow up."

"Thank you, Tyler, for that astute observation," I said.

She winked. "Anytime."

Thanks to a missed field goal, we made it to overtime and won on a long pass to K.J., who caught the ball and practically barreled over two defenders. Our side went wild. All my kids started hugging one another as though we'd won the lottery. Dylan clapped wildly, and the other football coaches' wives cheered because we'd have a calm week in the house.

Both teams lined up mid-field and performed their customary hand-slaps while saying "good game, good game" dozens of times. Then our band played the school song and the players began to head off to the locker room while the crowd drizzled down the stands.

Amber handed Dylan off to Skylar while she scampered to the bottom rail. I watched her eyes as she spotted K.J. Almost like telepathy; he looked up and caught her gaze. He flashed her a quick smile. She waved at him. He looked around—presumably to make sure my husband wasn't watching—then mouthed and motioned that he'd call her in a minute.

Quickly, my daughter pulled her phone from her pocket and held on to it for dear life.

The schoolgirl giddiness in her eyes brought water to my eyes. Now that J.D. was no longer an issue, it still seemed that my daughter was far too quickly getting attached to another boy—another one of my old patterns at work in her life.

Thankfully, my husband kept the boys super late, so late that Amber knew not to even ask if she and K.J. could go out that night. But apparently, he did text her later and asked if they could go out Saturday evening.

"We'll have to see what Darren says," I told her when she knocked on my bedroom door and requested permission.

"So...do you have something against K.J.?"

"No. I just don't want to see you fall too fast," I warned her.

She smiled. "But I *really* like him."

"But he's *really* still in high school, and you're *really* still nineteen, and your priority is *really* raising Dylan and doing *really* well at your new job."

"Oh my gosh, Mom, you are *so* raining on my life-parade."

"I was right the last time you accused me of being negative, correct?" I reminded her of the craziness with J.D.

"Yes, but that was the person formerly known to me as J.D. I've moved on now."

"Moving on doesn't necessarily mean moving into the arms of the next man. It's called rebound."

"It's not like we're engaged. We're just two people kickin' it. That's all."

I sighed. "Whatever." I couldn't help but think that we'd just had this conversation about K.J. not very long ago. And then J.D. came back into the picture. And how we were back to K.J. again.

"Um…" she shifted her weight while still standing at my door, "if Dad says I can go out with K.J., will you watch Dylan for me? I mean, Skylar and Tyler will really be the ones watching him, but I'm asking you if you'll supervise."

"I suppose I could supervise *if* you're allowed to go."

"Thank you."

The part of me that still wanted Amber to have a childhood got all but chewed out during the women's meeting that next morning.

"That's like, early-grandmomma-no-no-number one," Quinnetta informed me.

"What?"

"Keeping your unmarried daughter's baby while she goes out on dates."

There I was thinking I was talking about Amber's dating life when all of a sudden they were schooling me. "What are you talking about?"

"It's like this," Sheila said, "we don't want to punish young single mothers, but we do need to let them know that the baby is *theirs*, not yours."

"I—I just want her to have a *life*."

"She *has* a life—with Dylan," Sandra Jean said.

These people had me thoroughly confused. "What about the concept of not letting your children meet everyone you date? Isn't it better off for them?"

"Yeah, I suppose it is if you're an adult looking for long-term relationships, looking to get married. But take my word, Angelia, your daughter and that boy do not need to get to know each other all that intimately. Having baby Dylan around will definitely put a damper on any kind of romantic ideas on their date. Didn't your mother ever make you take your little brother on a date?"

They all busted out laughing, and I had to join, too. "I never had a little brother or sister, but I remember people who had to bring them along everywhere."

"Yeah. They were our birth control. Made us never want to have kids," Sheila joked. "No one's saying you need to punish Amber. We're just saying—let her feel the weight of her responsibility."

I won't lie: I was somewhat offended by their words. Sheila must have sensed my dismay.

After the meeting was over, she walked me to my SUV in the parking lot. "Hey, sis. Listen. You know your daughter better than anyone else. We're all just giving you our advice from our experience. You should talk to your husband about this, too. And ultimately, let the peace of God rule in your heart, okay? The Holy Spirit will give you the wisdom to know what to do in all things. No hard feelings?"

Had she not approached me after the meeting, I definitely would have left feeling some kind of way. But I knew Sheila's heart. It was full of love and compassion for both Amber and me. "No hard feelings, sis."

We hugged and parted ways with an unspoken understanding. These ladies were good people who always meant well. But like she said—I needed to hear God for myself on some things because so far just about all of the problems my family faced came out of left field!

Chapter 10

Darren and I talked and decided to let Amber go out with K.J. I knew the ladies from my church meant well but I felt in my heart things would work out well. Amber spent most of her childhood helping me with Demarcus so she never got a chance to hang out with friends. Being a single mom didn't mean that you couldn't have fun. Now don't get me wrong, I wasn't going to make it a habit of keeping Dylan every weekend while she ran the street. Amber and K.J. probably wouldn't have much dating time anyway due to his football practice schedule and Amber starting her new job at Ross.

"Mom, how do I look?" Amber asked as she entered the den. She had on some army camouflage leggings, a crocheted lace up poncho top and some black wedges. Amber had a wide bang and the rest of her hair pulled up into a cute bun. I had never seen my daughter so into her looks until now.

"I think you look cute, sweetheart."

"I know it's a little different for me, but my two stylists thought this was a good look for me." Amber giggled.

The twins came down the stairs. "Ms. Angelia, I think she looks hot. I hooked her hair up," Tyler pointed out.

"I picked out the outfit," Skylar chimed in.

I had to give them credit. "Well you guys did a great job."

"Okay, Mom, Dylan is asleep and probably will sleep all night."

"Here's his baby monitor," Skylar said. She handed me the monitor and I checked the volume to make sure it was on.

The doorbell rang and Amber's face lit up like a Christmas tree. "I'll get it," she sang.

"Naw girl, let the man come to you. You don't wanna seem desperate like you been waiting on him all day," Tyler said.

"Oh ok," Amber agreed but looked confused as to why.

My poor baby didn't have any experience with the do's and don'ts of dating. I'm certain Tyler had overheard Marcy or someone at school give advice on the matter.

"Tyler is right, sweetheart. I'll get the door," I said.

I walked to the door and let K.J. in and to my surprise, he had a nice bouquet of multi-colored flowers. He was wearing a nice pair of pressed jeans with a belt, a nice button down shirt and his letterman's jacket.

"Hello, Mrs. Holley, how are you today?"

"I'm fine, K.J., come on in."

I led K.J. down the hall to the den and Darren as well as Demarcus had joined Amber and the girls. Tyler and Skylar got googly-eyed when they saw K.J.

"Hey, K.J., glad you're here." Amber smiled.

"It's good to be here. You look nice," K.J. complimented her.

"Thanks, and so do you."

"Coach Holley, how are you doing?"

"I'm good, son, I see you brought me flowers," Darren joked, breaking the tension in the room.

"Um... no, these are for Amber," K.J. answered nervously. I could see the little beads of sweat on his brow.

"Well give them to her then," Tyler blurted out.

"Tyler, geez, let K.J. handle his own business," Skylar advised.

K.J. handed Amber the flowers and then shoved his hands in his jacket pockets.

"Thanks, K.J., they're beautiful," Amber beamed as she inhaled their scent.

"You two better get going so you won't miss your movie," I said, breaking the ice.

"Amber, I'll put your flowers in a vase for you," Skylar offered.

"What y'all going to see?" Demarcus asked.

"We're going to see the latest Furious movie," K.J. said.

"Ooooooh, can I go with y'all please?" Demarcus begged.

"Demarcus, you and I can go see the movie another time. Let's let your sister enjoy her date," Darren stated. He eyed K.J. "Remember the curfew."

"Yes, sir."

"Alright, K.J., let's go."

"Good seeing all of you," K.J. said as he and Amber headed up the hall and out the door.

I followed behind them and peeped through the window. I watched as K.J. opened the door for Amber and they pulled out of our driveway in his Blue Toyota Corolla.

Tears began to roll down my face.

"Babe, why are you crying?" Darren asked.

"I don't know." I sobbed.

"Angelia, people don't just cry for no reason."

"I guess because that's my baby."

"Babe, she's going to the movies, not the army." Darren laughed.

"I know it may seem silly to you, but I never got a chance to witness Amber going on a first date until now."

"I understand what you mean, but sweetheart, she's going to be alright. Amber has grown up a lot since having Dylan.

Don't worry yourself all night. She'll be ok." Darren gave me a reassuring hug. "I've got K.J. scared to even hold her hand."

"I guess you're right," I said.

"Mom, can we have our own movie night?" Demarcus asked.

"Yeah, let's do a movie marathon," Tyler added.

"I'll make the popcorn." Skylar hopped off the love seat and scurried to the kitchen.

"Ok, sounds good. Let's see what's on Netflix." Darren grabbed the remote and browsed through the movies.

"You guys go ahead and start the movie. I'm going to go and check on Dylan."

I went upstairs to the nursery. Dylan was still asleep. I even changed his diaper and he still didn't budge. I stroked his hair and kissed him on the cheek and went back downstairs.

Darren picked two movies for us to watch: *The 5th Quarter* and *Heaven Is Real*.

"Awwww man, I wanna watch something with some action in it," Demarcus whined.

"I was hoping we would at least get to watch one Tyler Perry movie," Tyler complained.

"Guys, these movies could be good. Let's just see," Skylar reasoned.

We watched both movies, enjoying quality time together. But my mind was still on Amber.

After the second movie ended, the children went to their rooms. Darren and I decided to stay in the den and wait for Amber to come home. He turned the TV to High School Scoreboard, a local TV sports show highlighting area football teams. We were both ecstatic to see The Lancing Springs

Tigers in first place in their division. We both let out a yell and high-fived one another.

I heard Amber walking up the hallway and my heart skipped a beat. I was glad that she was home. I couldn't wait to hear all about her date.

"Hey Mom and Dad, what are you guys so excited about?"

"The Tigers are in first place," I said.

"Oh that's great, I can't wait to tell Kevin."

"Kevin?" Both Darren and I said in unison.

"Yes Kevin, as in K.J. His name is Kevin Jr." Amber blushed.

"I know his name, just never heard you use it," Darren stated.

"Well from now on, that's what I'll be calling him."

I searched Amber's face: cheeks full from smiling, upturned lips, a twinkle in her eyes. Clearly she was already taken by K.J. I remember having that same look when I started dating Javar.

"I take it that you had a good time on your date?" I asked.

"Yes, it was great. Kevin and I had a good time."

"But I'm going up to check on Dylan. I missed my baby."

Amber left the room and headed upstairs before I could ask her any additional questions. I sat back down next to Darren and watched the rest of the show.

Things were starting to become clear to me. Amber is not a baby anymore she's a young adult. The best thing for me to do is to get a hold of my nerves and release her to God and let Him lead, guide and direct her like only He can. I silently prayed and released Amber to God, asking Him for a hedge of protection over her and Dylan. After praying I felt a little more relaxed about her new friendship with K.J. Excuse me—Kevin.

Chapter 11

The next morning we overslept so we missed church. I don't know why I didn't hear the alarm clock go off. I rolled over and noticed that Darren wasn't in bed. Our bathroom light was on and the door was open. I approached the door and saw Darren on the phone. I wasn't sure who he was talking to, but from his tone I could tell it wasn't a pleasant call. Darren entered the bedroom with a frown on his face.

"Honey, what's wrong?" I asked.

"That was my mom's nosey neighbor, Henry on the phone telling me that Mom has moved to a senior home."

"You just cut her yard not too long ago. Why didn't she tell you herself?"

"My point exactly. This is ridiculous," Darren fumed.

"Well, did he tell you the name of the place or where it's located?"

"Yeah, Lakeview Estates. On the north side of town. Mom and I had talked about her moving there after my father died. She had thought about selling the house then, and I offered to cover the difference between her income and the rent to help her stay there if she wanted to, but she wouldn't hear of it at the time. I guess she changed her mind. Won't be long before she needs help with the rent—it ain't cheap. But at least I know if I pay Lakeview directly, her basic needs—shelter, electricity, utilities and three hot meals a day—will be taken care of. My money won't be going toward the boat."

Though I wasn't crazy about this idea because I knew that Mother Holley would stop at nothing to get whatever she wanted out of her son, I also knew that I handled the finances in our household. If and when I put Lakeview Estates on auto-draft, that dollar amount would be a non-negotiable, done deal. "Honey, I think you should go there and talk to your mom."

"I need a few days to calm down before I do that. As a matter of fact, I'm headed to the gym; I need to clear my head." He tilted his neck to one side and then the other. Both times, there was an audible cracking sound.

"Ok baby," I said, giving him a hug and a kiss.

When Darren left I jumped up and threw some clothes on. It was time for me to pay my mother-in-law a visit. We needed to have a woman-to-woman talk. In the words of Shirley Brown: *Barbara...this is Shirley...* This mess between her and Darren would have to end today. I didn't like seeing my husband look beat down.

I pulled up the address on my phone and retrieved the directions to the senior home.

When I arrived at Lakeview Estates I saw it was a gated community that looked like an upscale apartment complex. Of course I wasn't surprised, because Mother Holley always had to have the best of everything. The grounds were well-manicured and there was a beautiful water fountain displayed near the entrance of the facility.

Before getting out of the car, I sent Amber a text telling her I would be back soon.

I walked to the information desk and noticed a brochure of weekly events. Every activity you could think of was listed. They even had a spa, a dry cleaner, a beauty parlor and a movie theatre. This place was unbelievable.

"Ma'am, how can I help you?" An attendant with a name tag that read "Flo" asked.

"Yes, I'm looking for my mother-in-law. Her name is Dorothy Holley."

"Ms. Dorothy is in room 112. Please sign your name on this sheet." She pointed to a clipboard that had a form attached.

"Sure." I signed my name and Flo pointed me in the direction of Mother Holley's room. I walked toward the room and stopped before knocking on the door. I had no idea what I was planning on saying. I took a few deep breaths and knocked on the door.

"Come on in, it's open," Mother Holley announced.

I entered the room, which was much smaller than I'd imagined it would be in such a grand building. She must have chosen a small studio plan because her sitting area, bed, and kitchenette were all visible from the entrance. There were only two doors inside, one probably for a closet and the other I assumed was a restroom.

Mother Holley was sitting in a chair with a black & white striped duster on with matching house shoes and headscarf. Mother Holley usually wore the latest fashion, so her attire truly shocked me.

"Hello, Mother Holley, how are you doing?" I asked.

"Oh it's you. I was expecting someone else." Clearly she was disappointed. She focused on her flat screen television.

"Look, I know I am not your favorite person." I said, trying my best to not get ugly with this woman. She kept staring ahead at Judge Judy as though I weren't even in the room. I lifted the remote control from her coffee table and pushed the mute button. *Oh, you will talk to me this day.*

"How dare you? I was watching that!"

"You can watch the re-runs at four. We need to talk *now* about Darren."

That got her attention. "Darren... what about Darren?" She widened her eyes, trying to act innocent.

"Mother Holley, you are indeed a piece of work. Why would you have Henry call Darren instead of calling him yourself? You are his only living parent. How dare you treat him as if he doesn't matter," I vented, crossing my arms and letting all my weight fall to one hip.

"Angelia, who are you to tell me what to do with *my* son?" she said sarcastically.

"I'll tell you who I am. I am a caring, loving, concerned wife, who hurts when her husband hurts. That's who I am," I said on the verge of tears.

"Angelia, I—" Before she could get another word out, she started coughing like she had tuberculosis.

"Are you ok? Let me get you something to drink." I rushed into the kitchen area and grabbed a bottle of water from the refrigerator.

"Here." I watched as she slowly gulped down the water, noticing that her hand shook.

But at that moment, I didn't care if her hands shook all the way off her arms. It was time she and I had it out once and for all. I guess I thought the only way I could get a word in edgewise was to give it a shot while she was occupied with the water and the last of her coughing, so I spoke my peace. "Darren has been trying his hardest to be a good son, a good husband, and a good father, a good coach, and a man of God all at the same time. He's stressed out."

Mother Holley held out her hand to stop me, but I rambled on seeing as she still hadn't caught her breath completely.

"Now, I've made the decision to stop complaining and being bitter about what he's *not* doing, be grateful for what he *is* doing, and help him where he falls short because if I keep pressuring him more and more, it just makes him withdraw more and more. At this rate, he won't make it to 50. If you lay off your extra demands as well, we'll both have a much happier Darren to deal with because at the end of the day, we both want what's best for your son."

"I give up, Angelia, I am not going to argue with you anymore. You're right and I am wrong." Mother Holley began to pant as if she couldn't catch her breath.

Wait a minute... did she just say I was right and she was wrong? I sat down and pulled up the only available chair in the room. I was in total disbelief.

"I've been mistreating you out of jealousy. But after seeing you today, I now know you must love my son with all of your heart. I hope you'll forgive me for my behavior."

The sound coming from my throat must have been like Scooby Doo when he was confused. *Ungh?*

Mother Holley repeated, "I said, I hope you'll forgive me."

I swallowed. "Yes, I do love Darren and yes, I'll forgive you."

"Well, he'll be all yours soon enough. I'm glad to leave him in good hands. Angelia, promise me you'll take care of Darren when I'm gone?"

"Gone? Where are you going?"

"Going on to be with the Lord. I have lung cancer, so my time here is limited. I've known for a while now, but promise me you won't tell Darren and promise me you'll take care of him."

My heart stopped beating, and my stomach began to feel queasy. Darren had already lost his dad. Now his mom? My heart ached for my husband.

I walked over to where she was sitting and placed my hands in hers as she talked. I felt a sting as tears formed in my eyes.

"Lung cancer." I heard the words but didn't want to believe them.

"Why didn't you tell us?"

"I didn't want Darren worrying over me. I have all of my funeral arrangements made so he won't have to lift a finger. I was trying to get him to take over the house without telling him everything. But I guess now that the city took it over for taxes, it's all the same. I've got enough to pay for the first few months at Lakeview. Shouldn't need more than that."

"Mother Holley, I don't know what to say." Tears began to flow down my face.

"Dear, there's no need to cry. I've lived a good life and I know where I'm going, so no tears. Just promise me you won't tell Darren."

"I can't promise you that. I don't think it's fair to keep this from him."

"Angelia, I've never asked you for anything. Please do this one thing for me."

I didn't answer.

"I have my insurance policy and funeral program in my drawer. Please take them with you so when the time comes, you'll be prepared."

Mother Holley acted as if she was asking me to care for a pet while she was gone on a trip. With trembling hands, I opened the drawer and retrieved the folder containing the insurance policy and funeral program. Everything was detailed, and the program was exquisite. Obviously, my mother-in-law was ready to transition. I wiped the tears from my eyes and sniffed to clear my nose. If she had accepted this already, there was no turning back.

I carefully eased the program and policy into my purse. "Alright, Mother Holley, I'm going to head on home so I can prepare Sunday dinner." I felt like I was outside of myself, watching someone play me in a movie. I didn't want to believe this was my life.

"Angelia, call me Mom." I hugged her tightly. We both cried.

I left the senior home feeling like I had weights on my legs. There was no way I could keep this from Darren. I got in the car and turned to the gospel station. Vanessa Bell Armstrong was singing Peace Be Still, one of my grandmother's favorite songs. I chimed in singing, *Whenever the Lord says peace, there'll be peace.*

I cried and prayed all the way home, asking God to give me the strength and the words to tell my husband. I know Mother Holley asked me not to tell Darren, but there was no way I'd be able to rest knowing he was unaware that his mother was dying. That's a secret I couldn't keep to myself. Darren deserved to know about his mom's condition. I'm sure he'd want to spend as much time as he could with her. I was making the right decision by telling him. Mother Holley would have to forgive me this time.

Chapter 12

I pulled into the driveway hoping Darren wouldn't be home so that I'd have time to figure out how I was going to tell him about Mother Holley, but he was indeed home. I don't think there's a right way to deliver this kind of news to anyone. I had to also consider Tyler and Skylar as well. Those girls were going to be crushed. Today would be a sad day in the Holley house.

I got out of the car and headed inside.

Amber was in the kitchen making Dylan a bottle. "Hey Mom, where have you been?"

"I had to go run an errand. Where is everyone?"

"The girls are in their rooms and Dad and Demarcus are in the den watching TV."

"Mom, what's wrong with you? You don't look well."

"I'm ok." I tried to pull myself together, but tears began to flow again.

"Mom, what's going on? Please tell me...you're scaring me. Should I go get Dad?" Amber panicked.

"No, don't go get your dad. I just need a few minutes to myself. I'm going upstairs." I wiped my eyes.

"Mom, clearly there's something wrong. Tell me," Amber demanded.

I looked at my baby girl's face and could see that she was not going to let me out of her sight until she found out what was going on.

"It's Mother Holley. I went to see her today and she's dying from lung cancer. She asked me not to tell Darren, but I've got to tell him," I confessed.

"Oh Mom, that's awful. Dad's going to be crushed."

"Be crushed about what?" Darren asked as he came around the corner.

My breath caught in my throat.

Amber hugged me and headed to her room.

"Honey, let's go upstairs. I need to tell you something."

"Ok, let me grab some juice and I'll be right up."

I went upstairs and sat on my bed and whispered a prayer, asking God to word my mouth and give me the strength to help my husband make it through this.

"Alright babe, what you gotta tell me? Which one of the kids did it?" He chuckled as he entered our bedroom.

"The kids are fine. It's about your mother," I said slowly.

"My mother? Oh boy, what did she do now? I don't even know if I wanna hear what she's done. If it ain't one thing it's another," Darren ranted.

"Darren, she hasn't done anything. I went to see her today and she...she..." I tried to get the words out, but they just wouldn't escape my lips.

"She what, Angelia? Spit it out," Darren said impatiently.

I placed Darren's hands in my hands and delivered the news. "Darren, she's dying from lung cancer."

"Lung cancer? Yeah right. This is some sick game she's playing to get attention," Darren said angrily as he pulled his hands out of mine and walked toward the restroom.

"Stop. Sweetheart, she's not playing a game." I reached for the folder with the insurance policy and funeral program in it and handed it to him.

He faced me again and took the papers from me. "Ok, so she gave you her insurance policy and had a program made. Classic. Enough is enough. This is unbelievable," Darren said as he scanned the information.

"Darren, this isn't a game. Your mother has cancer. She asked me not to tell you. Mother Holley apologized to me for being jealous and asked me to take care of you. She said she didn't want you worrying over her. I believe her, honey, she had a terrible cough and appeared to be weak; she was shaking. I couldn't keep this from you," I said.

Darren looked as if someone had just knocked the wind out of him. I hugged my husband and held on to him as if my life depended on it. Darren sobbed uncontrollably and plopped down on our bed. I rocked him like a baby.

I began to call on the name of Jesus.

"Jesus, help us. Jesus, I need you to pick my husband up and carry him through this. Jesus, give him strength, Jesus, give him comfort. Jesus, give him peace. Jesus, Lord Jesus, just keep your arms around us. Thank You, Jesus, I feel Your presence. Thank You, Jesus!"

We sat quietly holding one another for what seemed like an hour. God's presence was giving me the strength. I remember Sheila saying that if you call on Jesus your atmosphere will immediately change.

"Honey, thank you for not keeping this from me. I love you."

"I love you too and we're going to get through this just like we get through everything else," I encouraged him.

"I know we will and although we all have to die one day this is a hard pill to swallow. I remember Pastor telling us that God will give us peace and make us understand or something like that."

"Yeah, that's Philippians 4:7: And the peace of God, which passeth all understanding, shall keep your hearts and minds through Christ Jesus."

"I need to tell the girls. No need in waiting," Darren said.

"Those poor babies already have so much going on. We have court tomorrow and now this."

"That's right. The custody case is tomorrow. I almost forgot. Well we can't keep it from them."

Darren went to the intercom system and buzzed into the girls' room and summoned them to our room.

Both Skylar and Tyler entered the room looking confused.

"Whatever it is, I ain't do it," Tyler blurted out.

"Sweetheart, you're not in trouble," I said.

"Girls, I called you in here because I have something to tell you," Darren gasped.

"Dad, what is it? Please don't tell me we have to go stay with Mom again," Skylar pleaded.

"No, that's not it at all. It's your Grandmother Holley, she has lung cancer and she's dying." Darren's words sounded almost like a whisper.

"When did you find out, Dad?" Skylar asked with tears in her eyes.

"When can we go see her? This is real jacked up; why she gotta be smoking those stupid cigarettes? Dang man, this ain't even fair. Why she have to do this to us? Why we gotta keep losing people that we love? Why dad, why?" Tyler wailed.

Darren hugged Tyler and allowed her to cry on his shoulder.

This poor child had been through so much. My heart broke for her.

"Tyler, we haven't lost everyone. We still have our family and most importantly, we have God," Skylar added.

"I just found out today about Grandma. I will take you guys to see her soon," Darren responded.

"Alright Dad, we'll get through this. Love you." Skylar embraced him.

"Tyler, baby, are you alright?" Darren asked.

"I'm going to be ok. I just can't believe it," she mumbled.

"We are all in shock, but the word of God tells us that this day is coming. That doesn't make it hurt any less, but at least we know God will be with us through this process," I offered.

"Babe, let's get out of the house. I know you don't feel like cooking, so let's go out to eat," Darren said.

"Good idea. Girls, go ahead and get dressed and let Amber and Demarcus know we'll be leaving in the next twenty minutes," I said.

Both Tyler and Skylar hugged me and left the room.

I was glad that we were going out for dinner. I needed to get some fresh air and just be with my family in a different setting. When there is talk about death, it just makes you wanna wrap your arms around everyone that you love and care about.

Darren and I got dressed and all of the kids were ready to roll.

"Will someone please tell me what's going on?" Demarcus asked.

"Yeah. What's up?" Amber asked, bouncing Dylan on her hip.

"Grandmother Holley is sick, and we're not sure if she's going to make it," Darren said trying to be strong.

"Dad she's going to be fine, don't worry," Demarcus said and hugged him.

The children rode together in my SUV and I drove Darren's car. I knew he was in no shape to drive.

We decided to dine at a soul food restaurant called Mama's Back Woods Cooking. I had heard several people from the church talk about it and wanted to try it out. Needless to say the food reminded me of my grandmother's cooking. Being close to my grandmother reminded me of how sad it would be for Tyler and Skylar with Mother Holley.

After we ate dinner we went home and the Holley house was quiet. The children were all in Amber's room watching TV, Darren was watching a college football game in the den, and I decided to get some Bible study time in.

Monday mornings were always busy for us. I don't know why it took an act of Congress for the twins and Demarcus to get moving. Every Monday it was the same routine. I had to call them at least four times before they got out of bed. I finally got them up and out the door right before Mr. Lee, the bus driver, left them. My nerves were on edge because Darren and I were set to be in court to get full custody of the girls.

Darren and I drove silently downtown to the Lancing Springs Family Court.

I honestly wished I could've stayed home. I was in no mood to deal with Marcy and her drama, but I knew I needed to support my husband.

We caught the elevator to the second floor and walked down the hall to Court Sixteen as stated on the subpoena. The bailiff instructed us to sit on the long bench outside the court until our names were called. My nerves were all over the place. Darren must have sensed it, because he grabbed my hand and held it.

It's funny how just the touch of your spouse's hand can calm you. I couldn't help but stare at my husband. There I was all nerved up and he was trying to calm me down when he just found out his mother was about to die.

"What is it, babe? Why are you looking at me like that?" Darren asked.

"No reason...I just love you." I leaned in and lightly pecked his lips.

"Y'all need to get a room." Marcy walked up on us, breaking up our moment.

Now I know you don't have to dress up for court, but this girl needed her butt whooped for what she had on. Marcy wore a pair of capris, with a gold half-top, a black jacket and a pair of black and gold sparkling stilettos. I am assuming she thought the jacket would dress it up. She thought wrong!

"Holley vs. Reynolds, the judge will see you now," A court representative announced.

Marcy, Darren and I followed the representative inside of the courtroom. Marcy was on the left side of the room and we were on the right.

After being sworn in, Judge Melissa Woolwright proceeded. "Mr. Holley, I see you have a petition for full custody of twin girls, Tyler Renee Holley and Skylar Nicole Holley. Is that correct?"

"Yes, your honor."

"Mr. Holley, am I correct in saying that your wife, Angelia Holley, is their caregiver as well?"

"Caregiver? She ain't cared to give them nothing," Marcy said.

"Ms. Reynolds, please, no outbursts. I will get to you in just a minute," Judge Woolwright gave Marcy a side eye.

"Now Mr. Holley, back to you. Am I correct?"

"Yes, your honor," Darren answered.

"The petition that you have drawn up, Mr. Holley, states that you want full custody of the girls with no child support, and only supervised visitation for Ms. Reynolds."

"Supervised visits? I ain't no killer and I don't need nobody to tell me how to take care of my kids." Marcy's words slurred, followed by a loud hiccup, like she was Ned the wino from "Good Times". It was obvious that she had been drinking.

Judge Woolwright banged her gavel three times.

"Ms. Reynolds, let this be your last outburst. I will hold you in contempt of court. I know your emotions may be running high, but you've got to control yourself. I can't believe you have the audacity to come up in my courtroom drunk. Why in the world would you even think I would grant you custody of your kids?"

"The document states that your apartment caught fire and you were arrested for being drunk and unruly. You obviously have an issue with alcohol. I am sentencing you to rehab for three months. After your completion we'll then discuss if you can have visitation. Mr. Holley, I am granting your petition for full custody with a review in three months to discuss visitation."

"You can't take my kids! They all I got! I will die without my girls. I promise I'll do better!" Marcy cried and yelled.

"Bailiff, take Ms. Reynolds into custody," Judge Woolwright ordered.

"Mr. and Mrs. Holley you're dismissed." She banged her gavel and left the courtroom.

I was shocked at how quickly everything ended. Sandra Jean had told me that Judge Woolwright was a tough cookie and didn't tolerate foolishness.

Our victory to getting full custody of the girls for me was a bittersweet one. Being a mother I can't imagine being away from my kids. I prayed that whatever program the judge put Marcy on would help her get back on the right track.

"Well honey, it's over," I said.

"Yeah, I guess so. Let's go home," Darren said with a blank face.

I followed my husband down the hall and out the door to our car. I wasn't sure if he was still thinking about Mother Holley, or if he was concerned about delivering the news to the girls.

Chapter 13

I didn't know if I should give Darren some space to digest everything or try to get him to talk. My poor husband had been through a lot in just two days. I remember Quinnetta saying that she would just cover her husband in prayer when she was unsure about his feelings towards certain things.

The look on Darren's face read, *Leave me alone, I don't wanna talk about it.* As soon as we walked through the door he went into his office and closed the door.

We still had a few hours before the kids came home from school, so I headed to my room to take a quick nap. I decided to stop in and check on Amber and Dylan first. I softly knocked on the door and entered Amber's room.

"Mom, how did it go?"

"We got custody of the girls."

"That's awesome! Skylar is going to be thrilled."

"Yeah she will be, but I'm not so sure about Tyler." I sighed.

"I think she'll be ok, Mom. Trust God for it," Amber encouraged me.

"You're right. God's got this."

I noticed Amber was dressed and ready to go somewhere.

"Where are you going, all dressed up?"

"Mom, I wouldn't consider a pair of slacks and this top 'dressed up.' I have to go to work today for training. Did you forget?"

"Oh yeah that's right; I did forget. What time do you have to be there?"

"I have to be there at noon and it's over at four."

Dylan was trying his best to get out of Amber's bed. That child rolled until I caught him.

"Bah bah bah bah," Dylan said and pointed to his bottle sitting on the table.

"Oh, Mimi's baby trying to talk? You want your bottle?" I gave Dylan his bottle and he began to drink his milk. He moved my hand, showing me that he knew how to hold the bottle by himself.

"Amber, we've got to start giving him his cup."

"Say, I ready for my cup, Mimi, yes I am," I cooed.

Dylan laughed and continued to drink his milk, which was half gone.

"Ok, Mom, I've got to get out of here. I'll be back right after training. Bye, Mommy's little man. Be good for your Mimi." Amber reached over to give Dylan a kiss and he formed his lips to kiss her back.

"He'll be fine. He's a good baby, aren't you Dylan?"

Dylan smiled and nodded his head in agreement with me.

Amber and I both laughed.

Amber left and I took Dylan to my room. So much for my nap.

I turned the TV on, but couldn't find anything worth looking at. I refused to let my grandson watch or hear a bunch of arguing and strife.

Dylan and I made our way to his nursery and sat on the floor to play. The nursery was filled with too many toys that made noise. All of that squeaking was bound to get on my nerves, so I settled on the old school roll the ball game. After I realized that Dylan was only going to hit the ball, I put him in his swing. By the time an hour had passed, Dylan was knocked out.

With Dylan tucked away in his bed, I took the baby monitor and headed to prepare dinner before the children came home.

Another hour passed and I found myself pulling the dinner dishes from the shelf and setting the table gave me joy. I was excited about us dining together again. There's truly a blessing at the table. My chicken was baking, broccoli and rice were steaming, and I'd cut up all of the vegetables for my tossed salad.

While I waited for the dinner to finish cooking, I went into the den to watch TBN. I tuned in just in time to catch the last few minutes of Bishop T.Z. McKinney's message entitled "Hold Your Peace, God's Got You." He referenced Exodus 14:14, *The Lord will fight for you, and you shall hold your peace.* In his message he stated that when we feel weary, overwhelmed, and under attack, God is on the job working things out. We have to remember that we're not going into battle alone. We're going with the God who spoke everything into the universe. The same God who spoke to the wind and said peace be still, He never loses. Even when it looks like we have been defeated we have the victory in Christ Jesus.

Bishop was really preaching and I enjoyed every minute of it. He closed the message out by saying no matter what's coming against you, keep pressing into God. Put His Word first place in your life. Honor Him in all that you do. Let Him fight your battles and bring you into the land of victory He has prepared for you.

"Angelia honey, this rice is boiling over," Darren yelled from the kitchen.

I was so into the message that I forgot that I was cooking. I ran into the kitchen praying that none of the other food was in jeopardy of burning.

"Thanks babe, I got caught up watching Bishop T.Z. McKinney."

"McKinney...that name sounds familiar. I think that's the name of the pastor who's coming for our men's retreat. Is he from Florida?"

"Yeah, that's him. What retreat?"

"The brothers at church told me about it. It's coming up pretty soon. At some lake out in East Texas."

"Honey, I think that's a great idea."

"I'm not sure if I will be able to go. Just depends on how things are going with Mom," Darren said, saddened.

I turned to Darren and hugged him and gave him a kiss. "I love you, babe and it's going to work out."

"I love you too and I can't imagine going through this by myself. Thanks for all you do. Not just for me, but for the girls, too. For everyone. I appreciate you."

Darren kissed me deeper this time and with more passion. I guess we didn't realize how hungry we were for one another. It felt so good to be in his arms again, we'd been so busy with daily life issues that we put ourselves on hold. I made a mental note to try to plan a getaway for us soon.

"I appreciate you too, but I'd appreciate you even more if you would help me finish up this dinner," I joked.

"What do you want me to do?"

"I was kidding, dinner will be ready in about ten minutes."

The yelling coming from the hallway confirmed that the children had arrived from school.

"I hate him! I hate him!" Demarcus yelled.

Darren and I both looked at one another confused and rushed into the hall to see what was going on.

"Hate who?" Darren asked.

"My dad, I wish he wasn't my dad anymore."

"What brought this on, Demarcus? Did something happen?"

I shifted into Mom mode and prepared myself to pounce on Marcus if need be. *Did he go to my baby's school without me knowing? What's really going on?*

"I have been trying to call him for three days and he won't answer my calls or my texts, he don't ever spend time with me cause he don't care about me," Demarcus cried.

"Mom, Billy Washington rides the bus with Demarcus. He was bragging about going on a fishing trip with his dad and told Demarcus that his dad was a deadbeat," Skylar pointed out.

"Yeah, Billy better be glad he a lil' kid 'cause I woulda laid hands on him for real," Tyler added.

"Demarcus, your dad cares about you," I heard myself say, though I wasn't even sure if Marcus cared about himself, let alone anyone else.

"Mom, can I please change my name to Holley so I won't be an outsider?" Demarcus begged.

"Demarcus, you are *not* an outsider. You are a part of this family just like me and Tyler, right Dad?" Skylar stated.

"Right," Darren agreed. He bent down to face Demarcus eye-to-eye. "You'll always be my son, Demarcus."

He hugged Darren with all his little might. "Thank you."

Darren rose and addressed the twins. "Speaking of being a part of this family, we went to court today and the judge granted me full custody." Darren said, mainly looking at Tyler.

"Awesome, that's the best news I've heard all year," Skylar beamed.

"So does that mean we can't see Mom?" Tyler asked.

I looked at Darren waiting on his reply. The last thing we needed was for Tyler to go off.

"No, you'll have supervised visitation with your mom after she comes out of rehab. The judge felt this was the best decision for you both."

"I'm glad they put her in rehab 'cause my boy, Shorty mom died from some liver disease 'cause she stayed drunk," Tyler said, shocking all of us.

"So you're ok with me having full custody of you?"

"Umm duh... you are my daddy." Tyler laughed.

"See that's not fair. I want my name to be like Tyler and Skylar's, Demarcus Anthony Holley," Demarcus said with pride.

"Son, it's not that easy to change your name. There's more to it than you think. I know right now you're angry with your dad and trust me, I understand. We can't just change your name," Darren said.

"Well will you think about it?" Demarcus pleaded.

"Yes, your mother and I will take everything into consideration. But like I said: You are my son, no matter what," Darren reiterated.

"Group hug," Skylar said.

We formed a circle and hugged. I smiled toward heaven and thanked God.

Six Weeks Later

Chapter 14

When I got the invitation from *Hope for Tomorrow* to attend Marcy's "Milestone Marker" in the mail, I wasn't sure what to think. Was it a graduation? An intervention? A celebration? From what I knew of addiction recovery, those who had been addicted to something said they would be in recovery for the rest of their lives, like an ongoing battle.

I waited for Darren to get home from work before saying a word. Once he was in, had eaten, and was preparing for bed, I read it aloud to him.

"I don't want to go," Darren had managed to utter while brushing his teeth in the bathroom after I finished reading.

"Babe, this is important for Marcy."

"How is she clean and sober and on the straight and narrow in—*what?*—six weeks?"

Lord knows I didn't want to talk bad about Marcy, but Darren had voiced my thoughts and skepticism exactly. Still, I tried to keep a positive tone. "It's just a milestone marker. Doesn't mean she's come to the end of her journey. But it's good to celebrate along the way. This is life, you know? Nobody's perfect."

Visiting Mother Holley at her facility over the previous month and watching her decline had been one of the most painful, yet purposeful experiences of my life. In fact, being around the elderly men and women at Lakeview gave my life new perspective. The Bible is right when it says that the days of our lives are like a vapor. Life is far too short to waste it holding on to grudges.

Too bad Darren wasn't visiting his mother as much as I was. He might have been able to learn that lesson, too.

Darren reiterated, "You can go to Marcy's party with the girls if you want to. I can't do it."

I had been praying for Darren to open up to me more, but he seemed to be closing himself off to me and the rest of the family even more than last year's football season. It didn't help that we were just about at the playoffs, where every game could be the last for the Tigers. The team's Facebook page was on fire with well-wishers and people from our small town who acted like their entire lives depended on the Tigers' success.

Darren must have been feeling that pressure, plus the situation with Mother Holley...maybe going to celebrate Marcy's achievement was too much to ask of him at that point. "No worries. I'll take them."

Since I was in charge of the family taxi and thus the family calendar, I made sure Tyler and Skylar didn't have anything to do the evening of Marcy's event. When they came home from school that day, I spoke to them privately in my husband's office.

"What's up, lil' Momma?" Tyler asked in her perky tone.

"Well, there's a celebration happening tonight and I'd like you two to attend."

Tyler threw her hands up and swayed her body back and forth. "Party! Party! Wait—it ain't no party if *you'll* be there. What's really going on?"

Skylar's worried expression got the best of her beautiful brown face. "What's the matter? Is it Grandma?"

Tyler gasped.

"No. Grandma is still with us."

"Then what is it?" Tyler asked.

"We got an invitation. To your mother's milestone event, marking her achievements over the past six weeks."

Tyler scoffed, "Six weeks? That's barely long enough to get a report card."

"Right," Skylar echoed.

Now, the old Angelia would have called it a night. The old Angelia would have said, "Alllllrighty then, if y'all don't want to go, I ain't gonna make you," and then tossed that invitation straight in the trash without a second thought.

But the love of Christ—the idea of how He reconciled me—pushed me to push them toward the woman God had allowed to be their birth mother. "Listen, Marcy will always be your mother. Right or wrong, this is her place in your life. She's not perfect, but she's trying. I think it would do you both good to keep the doors of your hearts open."

Tyler crossed her arms and slammed her back against the couch. Skylar rubbed her thighs with her palms.

"Leave it open just a little, maybe. And as you see her coming back to herself, you can open it wider."

"Or shut it all the way," Skylar added.

I nodded. "That's your choice."

Tyler sat up straight and raised an index finger. "Maybe it could be, like, a glass screen door. Like, we got the door open, but we got a screen 'cause we gotta see you act right first before you can get in."

"I think that's perfect, Tyler. Can you agree to a screen door, Skylar?"

She shrugged. "I guess."

Hope for Tomorrow was an old Victorian-style home complete with a wrap-around porch and a white picket fence. It sat alone at the end of a long, winding street that I nearly missed coming from the busy boulevard. Honestly, it reminded me of one of those bed & breakfasts in a women's magazine. The setting alone probably put the inhabitants at ease, apart from the hustle of everyday life.

"What is this? Little House on the Prairie?" Tyler balked.

I suppressed a laugh, wondering how this girl even knew the name of that show. "No. It's called Hope for Tomorrow."

Tyler replied, "Looks more like Memories from Yesterday."

"That's enough. We're here for your mother."

Skylar remained silent, yet wide-eyed, taking in our surroundings.

We followed signs directing us to park behind the house. Roughly ten other vehicles were in place. Somehow seeing other cars there put me at ease about coming to a place I'd never been, to do something I'd never done, with two young ladies who were probably unspeakably frightened.

I found the next empty spot. "Okay, girls. Let's do this."

Slowly, we exited the vehicle and walked toward the back porch, where a short, elderly woman dressed in jeans and a t-shirt greeted us. "Hello! How are you?" Her nametag read "Pat."

"Fine thank you," Tyler answered for us all as she glared at me with a look that said I-told-you-we-didn't-need-to-dress-up.

She was right, of course, but I'd already told them that it was always better to be a little overdressed than underdressed.

"We're guests of Marcy Reynolds," I said to Pat.

"Perfect. Go right on in," she directed me.

Inside the house, classical music played while people—some casual, some in their Sunday best—stood around drinking what had to be sodas and tea. I imagined that, at one point, our gathering space had been known as the "front parlor," with its open, welcoming architecture. Hardwood floors and a soothing olive green wall coloring with white baseboards and moldings gave the room a family, home-like feel.

Tyler spotted Marcy across the room sitting on a lounge chair. "Momma!" She yelled loud enough for people to notice. She dashed over to Marcy and embraced her. "Momma, I missed you so much!" Tyler began sobbing uncontrollably as she held on to her mother.

Marcy reciprocated, hugging Tyler more tightly than I'd ever seen her do. She kissed her cheek over and over again, declaring her love.

All the while, Skylar approached Marcy slowly, right by my side. Finally, she spoke when we reached the sitting area. "Hi, Momma. You stopped drinking now?"

"Skylar!" I tried.

"No, Angelia, she has a right to be angry," Marcy said, looking up at Skylar. "One thing I've learned in here is that we all have a right to our feelings, baby."

The loving tone of Marcy's voice struck my heart. Though her edges were rough and her lips were without a hint of color, Marcy had never appeared more beautiful to me than at that moment.

"Everyone! Thanks for your patience. We're about to get started," a lady in a red dress announced. "Participants, please take a seat by your guests."

I grabbed two folding chairs for Skylar and myself while Tyler scooted herself in close to Marcy on the lounger.

An attendant came around to offer us refreshments. I found myself wondering where the printed programs were, but I quickly reminded myself of the nature of this gathering. They probably didn't print many things with people's full names on them.

Once everyone had a seat, we were basically in a circle facing the speaker. It looked like there must have been eight participants, each had between one and five guests.

"Thank you all for joining us. My name is Helen."

"Hi, Helen!" almost everyone spoke her name as though they'd been rehearsing it.

She continued, "I'm the director of Hope for Tomorrow and I'm a recovering addict, sober for seventeen years."

"That's what's up! You 'bout that sober life!" Tyler cheered, though apparently this wasn't the norm. She lowered her head and muttered, "Sorry."

We are so out of place.

Helen bowed graciously. "Thank you. I imagine that's about as long as you've been alive."

The room laughed.

Tyler winked at me and whispered with delight, "You hear that? She thinks I'm *seventeen.*"

I shook my head.

"Today is a very important day. It's a day your honoree has been working for, preparing for, and even dreading. I can't tell you how many people walk away from *Hope for Tomorrow* because of *this* day. For some, this will be the first time they've seen their friends and family through an unclouded head in a long time. And it hurts. But we're glad you're here to help us through, to support us as we head into our 'after' selves. So, let's get started with David."

A man in his mid-30s with a head of bright red hair stood and yanked up his pants with his belt. "My name is David."

I was ready this time. "Hi, David."

"I've got my mom here." He could barely speak the sentence before he started tearing up. "And she's been through so much with me. I was addicted to crack. Had a good job, a wife, four beautiful kids. And then, after my best friend died, I started drinking. When the alcohol didn't cut it, I turned to marijuana. Then crack. And I got addicted. Lost everything. When I couldn't sell anything else, I stole my mother's stuff. But she never gave up on me. Mom, I just want you to know I wouldn't be standing here right now if it hadn't been for your love and this program. Thank you."

I should have brought my Kleenex. It was going to be a long evening.

Marcy was the fourth to take center stage. She stood and walked where both Helen and the others had stood. "Hi. My name is Marcy."

"Hi, Marcy."

"I've got my two daughters here tonight as well as my ex-husband's new wife," she explained.

There was a slight uproar in the room.

"Yes, I know it's different to bring your ex's next, but I don't know what I would've done it if it wasn't for her."

My hand flew to my mouth as Marcy continued, "A while back, my ex-husband got married. And that made me feel very alone. All the hopes I had about having a normal, happy family suddenly slipped away. And to make matters worse, he moved into a big, beautiful house with *her*"—Marcy pointed toward me—"and she was even more beautiful than the house."

Is she still talking about me?

"Anyway, I had always been a casual drinker. I mean, I'd get drunk once a month or so, but that was it. Until he got remarried. And he was happy in love with *her*. My girls were getting to know *her*. *Her* kids. Shoot, she didn't even have to work! It seemed like I was the only one left alone, struggling. So I started drinking every day when I got home from work to keep away the depression, to numb the pain. And I was so drunk I didn't even realize my new boyfriend was try to take advantage of my baby."

Marcy began to cry, and so did I. Skylar's arms slipped around my waist. I held her on one side while Tyler covered the other.

"Anyway," Marcy said, "when I found that out, I had a plan. It was an evil plan. I was planning to poison that man. Very slowly, so no one would find out. The only problem with the plan was I had to be around him in order to kill him. And because I was drunk all the time, I wasn't thinking clearly. Some days I wanted him dead, some days I wanted him back, some days I just didn't know what to think."

She took a deep breath. "But that was then. This is now. And in the middle of all my mayhem, this woman, *she* has stepped in and helped raise my girls when I couldn't. Back in the old days, in slavery times, women used to *have* to do it. But Angelia didn't have to. She could have refused to stay in our town. She could have told my ex-husband to take the girls to his mother's house. She didn't, though. She's taught my girls to be resilient. How to be young ladies. And most of all, the fact that she brought them here tonight shows me that she's teaching them how to forgive and love."

Marcy looked at me head-on and said, "Angelia, thank you. Thank you from the bottom of my heart."

The massive lump in my throat prevented me from doing anything except mouthing the words, "You're welcome."

Chapter 15

With football season nearing a close, Darren busier than ever. I'd taken the girls to see Mother Holley a couple of times but it seemed that every visit was somber. Amber and I did everything in our power to lift their spirits but nothing seemed to work. Skylar's usual upbeat attitude had disappeared and Tyler's wittiness was on hiatus.

Sandra Jean and Sheila both had been praying for me and sending me scriptures to reflect on daily.

My walk with the Lord was growing stronger and I was beginning to pray more because it seemed as if my household was being tested. Marcus hadn't called or reached out to Demarcus in months. Demarcus had tried to call but the number was disconnected. Then Demarcus had spoken with his grandmother and she'd informed him that Marcus had moved to Houston.

My poor baby cried for days, and began to cling to Darren. Darren and I had talked with Demarcus and discovered that he was afraid that Darren would leave too, because he was always gone. Thankfully, Darren was able to convince Demarcus that he would always be there for him and would always be his dad.

As I reflected on our situation, I couldn't help but remember the song we used to sing at my grandmother's old church: *Hold to His hand, God's Unchanging Hand.* I didn't understand it back then, but, oh, I understood it now.

Amber and I had planned a meeting with Javar for lunch at Luby's. I didn't want to go, but Amber insisted that I be present for their first official visit. Honestly, I didn't expect Javar to stay in constant contact with her, but he called or texted Amber at least twice a week and had even offered to send money for the baby.

I'd changed clothes about six times and my nerves were getting the best of me. I settled on a pair of jeans and a plaid button-down shirt. The old me would have found a cute, tight something to wear to let him see what he was missing. *Thank God for change and deliverance.* Breaking those soul ties was truly life changing. I no longer had feelings for any of my exes. Of course I cared about their well-being, but that was it... nothing more.

I walked downstairs to the den where I was certain the twins were. Demarcus was gone to the game with Darren. Every now and then the Tigers had a Saturday game, mostly for show and exposing the boys to scouts.

"Hey girls, Amber and I will be gone for about an hour or so. I made chicken salad last night so if you get hungry you can eat that."

"Ok thanks, Mom," Skylar said.

"Can we go to the mall or something when you come back?" Tyler asked.

"I think it would be great. Make it a girls outing. I'll stay home with Dylan."

"Go where?" Amber entered the den carrying the baby. Dylan had on a little baseball jumper and a matching cap.

"Look at you, little pooh bear, where you going?" Skylar cooed at him.

Dylan was laughing and drooling; he's such a happy baby.

"I was telling the girls that after we finish lunch you can take them to the mall and hang out for a while."

"Oh... ok, that would be great. It's been a while since we had sister time."

114

"Yeah 'cause you're always with *Ke-vin*," Skylar sing-songed, then laughed.

"You right, Skylar, she's on lock. Clink. Clink," Tyler confirmed, pressing her wrists together.

"Whatever!" Amber blushed beet red.

"Y'all so silly. Amber, let's get moving. Girls, we'll be back shortly."

"Ok," they said in unison.

Amber and I went through the garage and got in her Ford Focus. Darren and I found a good deal online and purchased the car for her. With all of the kids' activities and Amber working, we needed an additional car. Amber had been so helpful with picking Tyler up from church step team, Skylar up from choir rehearsal, and picking Demarcus up from soccer practice.

"Mom, I'm nervous."

"Why are you nervous? You've been talking to Javar every week."

"Talking to someone on the phone is different from seeing them in person."

"You have no reason to be nervous. Everything is going to be ok."

I wanted to believe that as well. The truth of the matter was that I had no idea how things would go, what Javar would say, what he was expecting to happen... I was clueless.

"Let's say a prayer to help ease your mind. Lord, we thank You for this day that wasn't promised, for this is the day You have made; we will rejoice and be glad in it. Lord, we ask that this meeting with Javar will be what you would have it to be. Lord, remove the nervousness and please let us both have an open mind and remain positive in Jesus' name I pray, Amen."

"Amen and Mom, thanks for coming with me."

"Sweetheart, you're welcome."

Amber pulled into Luby's parking lot and spotted Javar. Javar got out of the car with a huge smile plastered on his face as he walked toward our car. I hadn't seen him in years, but he still looked the same. He hadn't aged any, still a Morris Chestnut look alike. I silently thanked God again for deliverance.

My crew and I got out of my vehicle as he approached my side.

"Hey Angelia, it's so good to see you." He hugged me, catching me off guard.

"Good seeing you too," I managed to say.

"Amber, baby girl, how are you?" He embraced her and held on to her for a while.

"I'm doing fine." Amber smiled holding Dylan toward Javar.

Javar reached toward Dylan and tickled his chin. "Hey little man!"

To my surprise Dylan didn't cry. He leaned toward Javar, and Javar gladly scooped him up.

"Alright, let's go inside," I suggested.

We all went inside and went through the cafeteria line. It's been years since I ate at Luby's. I ordered the liver and onions with mashed potatoes, corn, fried okra, a roll and sweet tea. Amber and Javar both ordered chicken fried chicken, broccoli, rice and cheese casserole, sweet potatoes and cornbread. Dylan had an order of mashed potatoes with gravy. Amber cut up small pieces of her chicken to mix in as well. Dylan only had a few teeth so his chewing was limited.

"I am so glad you agreed to meet with me, Amber, I want to get to know you and Dylan."

"Thank you for not forcing the issue and giving me time to adjust," Amber said.

"I know you are probably wondering how I got out of jail so early."

I put my fork down and listened attentively, because I had been wondering but wasn't going to say anything to him about it.

"For years I appealed, trying to get out. I won't make excuses for myself, but I was young and stupid when things happened. I had a gun on me, but I wasn't the one who killed that cop. Granted I did pull the gun out, but it was Jaybo who actually pulled the trigger. All of those cops wanted me to go down. I had been selling drugs and running things in Marshall and they wanted to make an example out of me, so they all testified against me. Angelia, that's why when you asked questions about what happened, you never got a straight answer. Dequan and Terry both did a plea with the cops to get less time; the cops turned them against me. Anyway long story short, one of the cops, Officer Lopez, got caught up in some mess and the guys in the hood had something over his head so he resigned and helped get me out. I'm out because of my mother's prayers and Officer Lopez."

"Well that explains a lot. In my heart I didn't believe you killed that cop," I said.

"The only crime I committed was selling drugs, and every day I regret it."

"We all make mistakes. The good news is that God forgives us and we can move on, right Mom?"

"Right." I smiled at Amber. She was the spitting image of Javar.

Javar was darker than Amber but they had the same nose, eyes, and smile.

"Amber, I missed a lot of your childhood and it's my prayer that I can be a part of your adulthood. I would love for you and Dylan to come spend some weekends with me at Grandma Peggy's."

"I think we can manage to do that, depending on my schedule. I work some weekends."

"I also am here to support you financially if need be. Is J.D. still trippin' with you?"

I was surprised to hear that Amber had shared that information with Javar.

"He's upset about me dating Kevin, so he's not active in Dylan's life."

"Kevin, who's Kevin?"

"Kevin is K.J., Dad. I told you about him already."

"Oh ok, you lost me there for a minute. Don't worry about J.D., he'll get over that. You just make sure you get your child support from him. He owes you that."

I sat quietly because this side of Javar was new to me. I allowed him to give Amber fatherly advice. Although she'd become close to Darren, she needed her father as well.

"I wanna meet Kevin too, need to make sure he got his head on straight."

"Dad, he's a good guy."

"Is he, Angelia?" Javar asked with a raised brow.

"He's a good kid. Very responsible. I trust him." I smiled.

"I still wanna meet him," Javar said with a serious tone.

Amber and I laughed.

We finished up the lunch and Amber and Javar agreed to stay in touch. He also stated that he would come check K.J. out at one of the games. Javar thanked me again for coming and told me he was going to give Amber $400.00 a month to help toward Dylan. I told him it wasn't necessary, but he insisted that since he wasn't able to pay child support, he at least wanted to do something. I was so pleased with the meeting and glad that Amber had her dad back in her life.

That evening Amber, and the twins went to the mall to hang out and Dylan and I stayed home.

Darren and Demarcus made it home in good spirits because the Tigers won 28-0.

The next morning I thought I was dreaming when I heard the phone ring. Our house phone never rang and the fact that it was ringing at 3:00 a.m. sent me into worry mode. The only people that called us on that line were my relatives in Marshall. Darren rolled over and answered the phone. He sat straight up and turned the lamp on.

"What? When did this happen? I'm on my way." Darren barely got his words out.

He dropped the phone on the bed and headed straight for the bathroom.

Immediately I jumped out of the bed and rushed into the bathroom.

"Honey, what's going on? Who was that on the phone?" I asked, not really wanting to know the answer. Darren's eyes were bloodshot and he looked like he was in a daze.

"My...mom, she's... she's gone, babe." He grabbed me and held on tightly.

Darren collapsed in my arms, and we ended up on the floor. I had no words to offer him; all I could do was console him.

My insides were screaming, but God was keeping me strong for my husband. I silently prayed for God to carry Darren and the twins through this. With the help of God I was preparing myself to be my husband's rock.

"Honey, let's get dressed and go to Lakeview," I said, helping him off the floor.

Darren didn't answer. He walked to the closet and looked for something to put on.

I went into Amber's room to tell her what was going on. I didn't want to wake up the twins or Demarcus yet. We could tell them later.

I went back into our bedroom, threw on some sweats and one of Darren's t-shirts so that we could leave.

Chapter 16

I felt my heart racing the closer we got to the north side of town. We arrived and I jumped out of the car but Darren just sat there.

I walked over to his side of the car and opened the door. Reality must have set in because he was not moving, only staring at the building.

"Babe, come on. Let's go inside."

"I can't do this, Angelia. Jesus, help me!" Darren wailed.

"Listen to me, honey, Jesus will help you. He's right here by our sides even now. Lord Jesus, send Your strength, send Your comfort. Lord, wrap Your arms around us. Lord, we love You and we bless Your name, for it's all in Jesus' name. Amen. Come on, honey, you can do it."

Darren got out of the car and the closer we got to the door, the tighter he squeezed my hand.

Darren stopped at the lobby chair and sat down while I went to the front desk to let them know we had arrived. The clerk informed me that paramedics had already pronounced Mother Holley's time of death. At that point, we were waiting for the funeral home to come and pick up the body.

"May we see her first?" I asked.

"Of course."

I walked back to my husband and asked, "Babe, if you don't want to go in the room, you can stay here and I'll go."

"No, I have to go," Darren sobbed.

"Are you sure?"

Darren nodded and we proceeded to Mother Holley's room.

Mother Holley's room was extremely cold and dark when we arrived. The only light that was on was a weak lamp. The nurse must have sensed my eerie feeling because she flipped the light switch on.

Mother Holley lay in her bed peacefully, with a slight smile on her face.

Darren stood silently over her body. He held her hands and let his tears flow. I was so glad to see the attendants arrive from Heavenly Funeral Home. I don't know how much longer I could have watched my husband in this state.

The funeral home attendants told us that we could leave, but Darren wanted to stay. I understood his need to stay, but I didn't want him to witness them putting Mother Holley in that long black bag.

The attendants put Mother Holley in the bag and placed her on a gurney. Before they zipped her up, Darren kissed her and laid on her, sobbing uncontrollably.

I wrapped my arms around his waist and hugged him from behind. I had to finally pry him off of her.

After the attendants and I got Darren up, they rolled her body out the door.

"I need some air," Darren said, walking after them.

"Babe, wait, don't—"

One of the elderly nurses stopped me. "Here, sweetheart. You might want to read this all by yourself. I'm not sure what it contains." She handed me an envelope with my name written on it in Mother Holley's handwriting. "I'll make sure your husband gets some air, and I'll bring him right back."

I nodded to the nurse and she left the room.

I opened the letter and read:

Angelia if you are reading this note then that means I am gone on to be with the Lord. Please remember to take care of my son. My arrangements have already been made so there's not a lot for you to do. I want my service to be held on a Thursday morning at 11:00 a.m. I figure that way the people who take off and have to travel can be off until Monday. Also whatever you do don't let that sister of mine have nothing and don't let her run over you. I'm getting tired, Angelia. It's time for me to rest. Oh yeah make sure the funeral is at the Civic Center and I want you and the girls to wear blue like me. My dress is in the closet, it's been pressed already. My shoes and jewelry are in the hatbox on the closet shelf. I was going to wear that hat, but changed my mind. Get that cute silver, foxy bob wig, brush it out and let them put that on me. Don't have no wake, that's a waste of money and don't add nothing to my program. Tell my nurse, Celestine to call the caterer that we spoke about for the repass. Celestine got the check. Angelia, it's time for me to go. I love you, and I hate we couldn't spend more time together. Stay strong for Darren and the twins.

I'm going to rest with the Father now.

Mother Holley

Tears streamed down my face as I read the letter, but then I couldn't help but laugh. Mother Holley, even in her death, was running things.

The week went by so fast. I had contacted Darren's Aunt Mabel and her husband, Ray and sure enough, Aunt Mabel was ready to get whatever she could, just like Mother Holley had warned.

"Ummmmm Angie, what you gonna do with Dorothy Ann's furs?" she asked the day of the funeral.

"It's Angelia, and right now, we're only focusing on making it through the service and also, Mom left me specific instructions about what to do with her stuff."

"Well I'm sure she told you not to leave me nothing... old mean heifer," she said, rolling her eyes.

"Aunt Mabel, this isn't the time for you to be bad mouthing my mother-in-law. My husband is about to lay his mother to rest. Either you're going to respect that or I am going to have to ask you to leave."

Sandra Jean called everyone into the living room for us to pray with the funeral attendants as we prepared to get into the family car. The girls and I wore blue dresses as Mother Holley requested and Darren, Dylan and Demarcus wore blue suits and white shirts.

The ride to the Civic Center was a long one. Darren and I locked hands and exchanged glances but never spoke.

We arrived at the funeral and so many people were there. People were everywhere. Mother Holley's instructions were for us to view her body on the way in.

Darren and I went up first and I must say Mother was as gorgeous as ever. Her makeup was just right and that silver fox bob wig was beautiful. Both Skylar and Tyler were crying and hugging each other.

The service was beautiful. We only had one song, a resolution from the church and remarks from the President of The Ladies of Elegance, an organization that she had been a part of for several years. The eulogy was done by Bishop David Zion Crandell of The Full Word COGIC. He was the bishop of the first church Mother ever joined, and he preached a good sermon. The food for the repass that Mother ordered was great.

I was proud to say that everything she requested was done, and it gave me joy in my heart knowing that we made amends with one another before she left here.

Chapter 17

All my life, I've heard people say that you really need your family and friends to surround you when you lose a loved one. When my mother passed away, she was the only person I would have wanted around me. I felt alone and inexplicably sad when she passed. Claudia and Erica tried to "cheer me up" because they were teenagers and didn't know any better. I stuffed the pain inside and moved on with my life, which is exactly what I saw my husband doing in the days following his mother's funeral.

Once the visitors left and the church folks stopped dropping off food, our lives were supposed to return to "normal." I tried to just be there for my husband because I knew the pain of losing a mother firsthand. But Darren kept saying, "I just want to be left alone" anytime I caught him sitting in his car or staring out the window in his office. He still ate and went to work and took the trash out, but he wasn't "there" mentally or emotionally, and he wouldn't let me be there for him, either.

Things only got worse when Coach Minden fell ill, which I learned about at a football game when the announcer mentioned that the district's coaches, teams, and friends were all praying for Coach Minden in his absence. The crowds from both sides had applauded.

Though I had been sitting two rows up from his wife, I didn't want to ask what was going on with her husband. I just clapped like everyone else and then sat there wondering why everyone else in Lancing Springs knew what was happening at my husband's job except me.

When Darren finally made it home after the victory, I waited until he wound down to ask, "What's going on with Coach Minden?"

"He's sick."

"I figured that much, but what exactly is wrong?"

Darren slid beneath the covers on his side of the bed. "An autoimmune thing. I can't even pronounce it. But it's something he's had for a long time. It's finally catching up to him."

My husband quickly kissed me, then pulled the comforter up to his neck and closed his eyes.

I knew that meant he didn't want to discuss it anymore, but I needed some answers. "So, are you the head coach now?"

"Something like that."

"Are they going to hire another coach to help you? I mean, you're only one man. You can't do the job of two."

His eyes parted slightly. "It's too late in the season to hire someone else."

"Well…why didn't you tell me about this?"

He glared at me. "Really? I've got a lot on my mind lately, as you know. Carrying this football team is a breeze compared to the rest of my life right now." With that, Darren turned his back to me and went to sleep.

"Mom! Please hurry up!" Amber yelled. "Kevin will be here any minute. We don't want to be late for story time."

I rushed to finish changing Dylan's clothes while Amber changed in the bathroom. "I don't know why you're taking my grandson to be around all those other germy kids. Make sure you clean the books he handles with an antibacterial wipe. And is K.J. okay with being around all these kids?"

"He doesn't mind. He has a lot of cousins so he's used to children, but he may not be so good with baby messes."

Only a few minutes earlier, just when Amber was about to head downstairs with Dylan to wait for Kevin, Dylan had spit up all over Amber and himself.

"Well, I told you I thought he was allergic to peaches! They bothered his stomach last time, too."

"Okay, okay. Now we know." Amber breezed back in the room wearing a fresh shirt, smelling of her strawberry-scented body spray.

Dylan giggled when he saw her.

Amber smiled at him. "And *you*, little boy, have to stop regurgitating on people."

Dylan was tickled to have her attention. He gurgled all the more, flashing his new teeth.

"Comes with the territory," I said, handing her the baby and his diaper bag.

"Oh my gosh, Mom, I hope he doesn't throw up on Kevin."

I shrugged. "Well, if Kevin—or anyone you date in the future—wants to be with you, he'll have to adjust to Dylan as well. You two are a package deal now. A *great* package I might add."

The doorbell rang.

"Bye, Amber!" The twins yelled as she swished past the game room. They were engrossed in some reality show.

"Bye!"

Amber held on to Dylan with one arm and the stair's railing with the other. She had the baby bag on her left arm, her purse on the right. Far from the carefree image most people have when they think of a young woman going off on a date with a young man.

Just watching her as I followed her descending the staircase brought back my own memories of being a single mom searching for Mr. Right.

I reminded myself, You are not Amber and Amber is not you.

Demarcus, who was sitting on the couch playing his handheld video game, glanced up momentarily. "You look nice."

"Thanks."

"I was talking to Dylan." Demarcus busted out laughing at his own joke.

Amber detoured and playfully popped her little brother on his head.

"Ouch!" He looked at me.

I smiled. "That's what you get."

When we reached the door, I opened it, thinking I would let Kevin in for a moment.

Sunlight streamed into the foyer.

"Hi, Mrs. Holley."

"Hello, K.J." I looked past him and saw a Toyota sedan. "A new car?"

He looked over his shoulder as though it would have been a surprise to him, too. "Oh, no ma'am. I borrowed my cousin's car so we would have room for a car seat. She has a son about Dylan's age—we'll use his seat."

"That's very thoughtful of you, K.J."

"Thank you."

Amber kissed my cheek. "Bye, Mom. We have to go."

"Well, okay. I guess."

"Bye, Mrs. Holley."

"Bye, you two. Have a great time at the library."

Again, I watched as K.J. walked my daughter to the car.

Amber said to him, "You won't believe what happened. Dylan got sick all over me."

"Dylan! Good job, buddy! Two points!" K.J. rustled Dylan's hair and the baby smiled. Somehow, Dylan seemed pleased by K.J.'s roughness—must have been a boy thing.

"No you didn't!" Amber shoved K.J.'s arm.

Together, they got Dylan settled in his seat. Their beaming smiles and flirty actions confirmed what I already suspected: They were falling in love.

"Lovebirds," I whispered to myself and sighed. "No need trying to fight it."

Though I never would have told Amber, I was extremely happy for her. Come to think of it—with my husband working enough for *two* men and my house filled with kids doing their own thing—I was actually close to being jealous of Amber. Who wouldn't be? She had someone to spend her Saturday morning with. Someone to laugh with, even someone who had already begun helping her with her son.

She had everything I thought I had with Javar. And Marcus. And Darren. True enough, Darren was different. He wasn't a drug dealer, he wasn't a cheater, he had a good heart and he was a good provider. But he was a competitive workaholic. Worse than that, he was a competitive workaholic who shut down and sought distractions when he was grieving.

Where does that leave me?

I guess I called myself creating my own distraction by cleaning up the house. I pulled out my buckets, chemicals, and rags and started sweeping and mopping floors, disinfecting cabinets and toilets. Though I had done this all before in preparation for visitors after the funeral, I suddenly felt like doing it again. Couldn't do any harm to wipe the extra germs away.

While wiping and sloshing warm water everywhere, my mind went into autopilot mode as my thoughts drifted back to what it felt like to be giddy-in-love. I remembered one time when Darren and I were dating, we went to a drive-in movie theater in some small town south of Dallas. We'd parked the SUV, opened the back part and made a little picnic for two.

Those were the good old days.

Chapter 18

Our Tigers lost their last game of the season 24-20. I don't know how we let the Eagles beat us like that, but they won fair and square.

My kids were distraught in the stands, holding on to each other as though we had lost the family dog. On one hand, I was heartbroken for my husband because this time, they had gone one round further than last year, only to be defeated one game away from the state championship.

On the other hand, just like the previous year, I was relieved that the season was over. I could have my husband back and the kids could have their father back now for the next six months. Hopefully, Coach Minden would return or the school would hire a qualified coach to assist Darren next year.

Only a month had passed since Mother Holley's death. My husband was still in silent mode. He had even gotten a little snappy with the kids and me, which I understood as part of the grieving process. If he didn't come back to himself in the next several weeks, I would have to try to convince him to go to counseling so he could process his feelings.

Thankfully, the Lord heard my prayers. Just so happened that on Darren's first free weekend, the men of Mighty Move of God Worship Center had a retreat planned. For weeks, the brethren had teased my husband and told him they wouldn't dare register him because they were counting on him being in the championship.

But now that he was clearly out, Pastor Watkins called the house Thursday evening to talk to my husband.

"I'm sorry, Pastor, but he's not here at the moment. They're finishing up some business at the school. Taking inventory of equipment and such."

"Yes. This year was hard on your husband, you know?"

I wasn't sure how much my pastor knew, so I simply said, "Yes, sir."

"I've been talking to him."

"Oh?"

"Yes. We men don't tell y'all everything, you know?"

"Apparently not."

Pastor laughed. "Darren's a good man. Solid. He's glad to have you, and the church family is glad to have all the Holleys in our congregation."

"Thank you, Pastor. We're glad to be members. My girls love the dance team and the choir, and of course they're head-over-heels for Miss Earlene."

"Oh, yes. Miss Earlene is everybody's favorite," he agreed. "If you don't mind, please tell your husband to give me a call when he gets in. I've been trying to get hold of him but didn't get a response."

"Well," I ventured, "Darren's been…kind of quiet lately. Since his mother passed."

"Yes, I know. That's to be expected. Just be patient with him."

"I'm trying."

"Keep on trying. And tell him to call me, please. We'd like to see him at the retreat. I think it would do him good."

"I sure will."

When Darren got back, roughly an hour after the kids went to bed, little did he know I already had his retreat bag packed.

"Honey, Pastor Watkins called. He wanted you to get in touch with him."

"Yeah. I saw his texts. They want me at the retreat."

I warmed Darren's plate in the microwave. "So...are you going?"

"Maybe."

You know, I really didn't want to try to manipulate my husband, but this man needed to get somewhere and talk to somebody or at least have the elders lay hands on him before depression or something even worse set in.

The microwave beeped and I set his plate down at the table along with utensils and a napkin. "If you hang around here this weekend, I've got a lot for you to do."

"A lot like *what*?"

"We need your help taking down the blinds so we can clean them. *All* the blinds. Upstairs and downstairs. I need you to dust on top of the armoire since you're the only one who can reach the top, and—"

"Woman, if I didn't know any better I'd think you were trying to force me to go to the retreat," he said staring up at me.

I dropped my shoulders. "Okay. You got me. I'm sorry, Darren, I just really want you to go to this retreat. You've been so uptight lately—"

"I just lost my mother," he interrupted.

"Baby, I know. It hurts. You *know* I know."

He shoved mashed potatoes into his mouth. Then he asked, "If I go, will you stop trying to make me open up to you and let me grieve my own way?"

"Yes. I mean, unless things start to get destructive. Then I'll have to intervene. You understand that, right?"

He nodded. "Fair enough. I'll go to the retreat. I've taken off work tomorrow anyway."

What?! A day off? I felt like hugging my husband, holding him, stroking his back and comforting him, but I knew he would have only shrank away as he had gotten into the habit of doing.

Instead, I sashayed over to him seductively. "When you get back, I'll have something special waiting for you."

He stopped eating. Raised an eyebrow. "Something special like what?"

His guess was as good as mine, but at least I had his attention. "You'll have to wait and see."

Darren dropped his fork and grabbed my waist. "Can I get a peek tonight?"

I poked out my lips and tilted my head as though thinking. "Mmmm...I could be talked into a preview tonight. But you won't get the full feature until *after* the retreat."

True to my word, he got the standard treatment that night, which was enough to light the fire in my heart again.

He left Friday afternoon for the retreat, which gave me some time to catch up with Sandra Jean and Quinnetta. I carved out a few hours Saturday to meet for pedicures since we were all husband-less for the weekend. It felt good to have a few hours to myself finally.

With our feet soaking in steamy hot water, glasses full of soda in our hands, and the chairs massaging our backs, we fell right into comfortable girl-talk. "I know you're glad the season is over," Sandra Jean said.

"You know it."

"Why didn't you want the Tigers to go all the way?" Quinnetta fussed. "We haven't won a championship in eleven years!"

"Because I haven't had my husband in half a year!" I said. "Football season is so stressful on us. And to top it off with Mother Holley dying…"

Sandra Jean scoffed, "It ain't like the woman tried to die."

The way I said it must have sounded crazy. "I didn't mean it like that. I suppose there's no good time to lose a loved one. It's just…sometimes I feel like marriage is a big, huge obstacle course. You never really reach the end of it. And as a woman, it's like my real job is to just…help."

"And your problem is?" Sandra Jean asked.

I sloshed my feet in the water. "The problem is that I didn't sign up to be a helper. I signed up…to love and be loved, to cherish one another, to feel like there was someone who always had my back."

Quinnetta asked, "You don't have that now?"

"No. Not this very second. My husband isn't here for me now because he's grieving. And when he's not grieving, he's into football. Now, when he's not grieving and it's not football season, we're in business. Do you think I'm being selfish?"

Quinnetta nodded. "Most definitely." I could always count on her to be honest.

Sandra Jean intervened, laughing, "Now wait a minute. You feel what you feel. Right?"

I eyed Quinnetta, who rolled her eyes.

"Right."

Sandra Jean slapped Quinnetta's hand. "Stop, girl."

Quinetta took a sip of her soda. "All I know is, you've got your health and strength, a sound mind, a good man, good kids, a beautiful home, and you ain't got to work. You're blessed more than you know. Focus on being grateful."

Her words shut my lips tight. She was right. This time three years ago I would have given my right arm to be where I was just then, sitting up in a nail salon with true friends, getting pampered while my husband was on a retreat with the brethren from our church and our children were relaxing at home in our six-bedroom mini-mansion.

"You're right, Quinnetta."

"I say find you some scriptures on contentment, too," Quinnetta said. "I'm not trying to be funny, but you're on your third marriage. It's high time you learned that it's not so much about the man as your *perspective* on the man. In my opinion, as long as you're not dealing with a maniac, an abusive man, or somebody just outright making a mockery of holy matrimony, you got to learn to work through all these different seasons or else you'll just be hopping from man-to-man all your life."

"I know, but—"

"Didn't you learn that by your second husband?" Quinetta continued. "Let's back up. Remind me again, what happened with the first husband?"

"He went to prison."

Sandra Jean and Quinnetta busted out laughing. "Maybe my theory isn't airtight after all."

I shook my head at Quinnetta. "You know I have to just look over you sometimes 'cause you can't have no kind of perspective on a man who's locked up."

She caught her breath. "Yes, you sure need to. Lord, I forgot that man went to the pen! Didn't he get out, though? Is he...okay in the head?"

"Yeah," I admitted. "He's trying to stay in touch with Amber."

"That's good," Sandra Jean commended.

"Speaking of exes, my *first* cousin is dating my *first* love!"

"What?" they both gasped.

"Yes. It's crazy. He's divorced now. He reconnected with some people in our hometown. Next thing I heard, he had started dating my cousin." I gave my duck-lips.

"How do you feel about it?"

"You know, it's not like I *want* Sherman. I've broken that soul tie. I think it's just…I feel betrayed by her."

Quinetta tilted her head and shrugged. "Well, if you don't want him, and if he's already been through one marriage, after all this time he's probably not the man you knew. That may be a good thing."

"Well, I say to each his and her own." Sandra Jean held up her glass and we toasted. "Let the past stay in the past. Let's fast-forward back to now. With you and Darren. What I want to know is: What is your prayer for your husband?"

I thought for a second, then answered, "I'm praying that he will stop being so quiet, that he won't get on my nerves too much, that he will stop being such a workaholic and stop being so distant with the kids, and stop—"

"Whoa, whoa, whoa." Sandra Jean gave me the stop-sign with her hands. "You're not praying *for* your husband, you're praying *against* him. You're praying about all the things you want him to stop doing."

Confused, I asked, "What's the difference?"

"The Bible says call those things that be not as though they were, not call those things that you want to *not* be. The spirit world doesn't process 'nots' well. You have to pray *for* your husband. Pray that he will open up to you, that he will be the husband and father God has called him to be, that you will be the helpmate God created you to be. That's what I mean by pray *for*. Meditate on that. The Lord will make it clear to you."

We continued in bliss, getting our feet massaged and prettied up. We parted ways a few hours later, which gave me just enough time to drop by Victoria's Secret to pick up some new lingerie so I could make good on the promise I made to Darren before he left. My second stop was for bath and massage oils. I also threw a sleeping mask into my basket. *This should make things interesting.*

I spent the rest of the weekend praying for Darren. Pulling scriptures about comfort, peace, and drawing strength from the Lord. I even got the kids in on the action, telling them how much their father needed them right now. Tyler and Skylar admitted that they needed comfort, too, as they worked through losing their grandmother. They also wanted to pray for their mother's continued recovery.

When I tell you we were a scripture-searching people that Saturday, I mean that.

Sunday morning, the men returned from the retreat just as service began. They came into the sanctuary wearing T-shirts that read "A Changed Man" and from my husband's countenance, I could tell it was true. He walked into the sanctuary along with the other men as we sang the opening congregational hymn. Right in front of the kids and everyone else, Darren picked me up off my feet and swung me around in the center aisle!

Everyone cheered for us as Darren swung me twice and then gently lowered me back to a stand. That's when I saw the tears in his eyes. Quickly, my hand flew to catch them as they fell down his cheeks. "Baby. Are you okay?"

"I've never been better, Angelia. God is good. We have a wonderful life ahead of us, and I'm asking Him to help me enjoy every day of it with you."

"Awww…" those who were close enough to us cooed.

The truth is: I may never know exactly what happened to my husband during the retreat weekend. Maybe it's not for me to know. And honestly, I really don't care. All I know is that God answered my prayer. My husband came back with an improved attitude. Ready to face the new days ahead.

Not to mention he was more than ready for what I had in store for him that night.

Chapter 19

After spending time with Quinnetta and Sandra Jean it really got me to thinking. I was truly blessed. Darren and I were blessed beyond measure. I was so thankful for the retreat and the changes that God was making in Darren and in my marriage.

I needed to be completely whole again and part of me being whole meant that I needed to reach out to my cousins, Erica and Claudia. Those two were like sisters to me and there was no reason for us to go so long length of time without talking. Life is too short and with all that we'd been through it's not worth it.

I picked up my cell phone and dialed Claudia's number but then hung up. I had no idea what I was going to say. I couldn't say I forgive you for being with Sherman or you have my permission to be with Sherman. My phone rang, disturbing my thoughts and it was Claudia. I braced myself and answered.

"Hello."

"Hey, it's Claudia. I see I have a missed call from you."

"Yeah I called. I wanted to talk with you. We haven't talked since the mall."

"Ok, you got me. Talk," Claudia sassed.

"Claudia, the bottom line is that we're family, and I can't allow your relationship with Sherman to hinder my relationship with you."

"Well if you think I'm breaking up with him that's not happening."

"I'm not asking you to break up with him," I said, getting frustrated. Honestly I was shocked by her behavior. Claudia was treating me like *I* was the one in the wrong. Was I wrong?

It didn't matter about right or wrong. I needed to make things right with my cousin and move on.

"What are you asking me, Angelia?"

"I'm asking for your forgiveness," I said slowly, not knowing what she would say next.

"Angelia, I've already forgiven you."

"Thanks Claudia. I love you, you know. You're my sister," I said, in tears. A great burden had been lifted off of me.

"I love you too."

Claudia and I chatted for a few more minutes. The iciness between us melted, and we ended the conversation promising to talk again soon.

Although things went well with Claudia, I was unsure how Erica would be. Erica said some pretty harsh things to me. Knowing that Erica could be a tough case to handle, I whispered a prayer asking God to let the words that come out of my mouth be what He would have me to say.

Erica's phone rang three times before she answered.

"Who dis?" Erica answered, knowing dang-on well it was me.

"It's Angelia," I said calmly.

"What you want?"

"I called to apologize, Erica," I said, getting straight to the point.

"Well apologize, I'm listening," she huffed.

Clearly I am being tested, but the devil is a lie; I am going to pass this test.

"Erica, I apologize for the attitude I had when calling you about Claudia and Sherman, I pray that you'll forgive me."

"Good. You *should* apologize... is that all you wanted?"

"Yes, that's it," I said.

Erica's attitude made me feel as if she wanted to continue to fight; I wasn't interested in traveling down that road with her. Spiritually I knew better and knew that no good would come out of it.

"Aight then holla," she said and hung up the phone without giving me the opportunity to say anything else.

Oh well, that didn't go as I hoped it would, but I still had my joy. I remember my pastor saying that we are only responsible for our actions, not others' actions. Erica has always been rough around the edges and although I would love for us to make up, it was totally up to her. I'd done my part and I felt great.

I headed to my kitchen, pulled out a notepad and jotted down a few ideas of things to do for Thanksgiving. I wanted to do something special for Darren. This would be our first holiday without Mother Holley. Going on a cruise crossed my mind since the children were going to be out of school, but I knew Amber would want to be able to spend time with Javar, plus she really hadn't been working at her job long enough to request time off.

Darren didn't have any ideas or suggestions when it came to holidays; he basically left it up to me. This had truly been a trying year for us. We had so much to be thankful for.

"Hey Mom, what are you doing?" Skylar asked as she, Tyler and Amber entered the kitchen.

"Sitting here trying to come up with something for us to do for Thanksgiving. Do you guys have any suggestions?"

"Let's go skiing at a nice resort," Tyler said with excitement.

"No, we need to just have a big family dinner, because Thanksgiving is about being thankful and spending time with your family—your *whole* family," Skylar said.

"When you say *whole* family, who do you suggest we invite?" I quizzed.

"We should invite Mom, Claudia, Erica, Mr. Javar, Ms. Rose, J.D., Miss Earlene, and K.J. since they are part of this family too."

"Whoa, I'm not sure if it's a good idea to invite J.D."

"He's Dylan's dad, so we should invite him and leave it up to him to come."

"I think she's right." Amber's response surprised me.

"Are you sure about this, Amber?"

"Yes I'm sure. I don't have an issue with J.D. coming, and I am not worried about him bringing Nicole, because Ms. Rose confirmed that they broke up."

"What about him seeing you with K.J.?" I asked.

"Oh well, that's *his* problem. Amber has moved on, so he can just kick rocks as far as I'm concerned, he don't want none," Tyler said and punched the air.

"Alright Mayweather, calm down. There will be no fighting." I laughed.

"Mom, it will be ok and the girls and I can help cook the dinner too," Amber offered.

"Yeah, I'll be over the cranberry sauce," Tyler volunteered.

"Cranberry sauce," Amber, Skylar and I said and laughed.

"It's settled. We'll have the dinner and invite everyone over. I'll go purchase some invitations and mail them out tomorrow."

"Thanks for doing this, Mom, it's going to be great." Skylar hugged me.

"Alright let's work on the menu so we can go shopping," I said.

The girls and I spent the afternoon planning our menu. The menu consisted of a ham and a turkey from the BBQ house, greens, yams, corn casserole, green bean casserole, salad, peas, cornbread, pea salad, pecan pie, sweet potato pie, pound cake and cheesecake. We planned to serve punch, tea and water as our beverages.

The next couple of weeks went by really fast. The children had some time out of school and helped me clean the house and decorate the dining room table. I was excited to be hosting somewhat of a formal dinner at our home. Everyone with the exception of Erica and J.D. had responded to the invitation.

Darren had been in good spirits for the most part about the dinner, but I could see there was still a sadness in his eyes. I was praying that having family over, eating, laughing and watching the Dallas Cowboys would help him make it through the day.

The girls and I had been up all night slaving over the stove and were ready to greet our guests. Tyler suggested that we wear brown sweatshirts with the words "Give Thanks" on them with a picture of a turkey on it. She had been surfing the Internet and saw the shirts. I ordered shirts for all of us, including Dylan.

With all of the cooking we'd done the night before, you'd think I wouldn't want to cook breakfast. I still wanted our family to do something special before our guests arrived, so I prepared a light breakfast casserole with eggs, cheese, sausage, onions, and bell peppers. I summoned the family to come to the kitchen table for us to eat.

"I'd like to start a new family tradition. I want each of you to tell what you are thankful for. We'll start with you first, Demarcus," I said.

"I'm thankful for all of y'all, this good food, and that I'm getting better in soccer and that Dad is my dad."

"Skylar, your turn," Darren said.

"I'm thankful that we're all together, that everyone is healthy, thankful for my good grades, for you, for Miss Earlene and our church family."

"Tyler, you're next," I said. She made a big production of rising from her seat and clanking a fork against her glass. She cleared her throat twice. "Hear ye, hear ye. I'm thankful that my mom is getting better. For my sisters Skylar, and Amber, for my big head brother, Demarcus, for my cute nephew, my dad."

Suddenly, the grin on Tyler's face fell and a somber expression took its place. Her eyes moistened. "I know it's been a hard year. In the beginning, I gave you a hard time. But you stuck by me through it all, no matter what I did." Her voice cracked. "So I'm thankful for you, too. Mom." Tyler quickly said and sat down.

Tears ran down my face hearing the word 'Mom' come from her lips. Tyler was right. She and I had come a long way, so hearing those words filled my heart with so much joy. I reached over and hugged her tightly.

"Wow, thanks for making me mess up my mascara, Tyler," Amber said jokingly.

"I'm thankful for our entire family and I'm thankful for my son. Dylan has brought so much joy into my life and I'm also thankful that I finished my home school program and got my diploma. I'm thankful that I can now focus on getting a degree and providing for me and my son."

Next, it was my turn. "I'm thankful for my wonderful husband. Honey, you mean the world to me. You take such good care of us. Thank you for adding to my life and for bringing these two beautiful girls who I'm proud to say are my daughters. Amber, I am so proud that you finished high school and you've given the most handsome grandson in the world. Tyler & Skylar, I'm so proud of how courageous you both have been throughout this whole process. It's not easy being part of a blended family. You two are turning out to be wonderful young ladies, and I'm honored to be a part of your lives. Demarcus, I'm so proud that you're turning into a wonderful young man. You don't let your struggles stand in your way. You brought that C on up to an A, and I knew you could do it! I am so proud of you all. Our blended family has been through so much, but you guys hung in there together and we made it work. I love y'all."

Finally, it was my husband's turn. "Babe, you give me too much credit; you take care of all of us. Thank you for the way you run this house, you make sure all of our needs are met. When my mom passed, I wanted to give up and throw in the towel, but you wouldn't let me. You have covered us in prayer and for that I'm thankful. I see the hand of God moving in your life, in all of our lives and for that I'm truly thankful. Amber, twins and Demarcus, you guys make me proud. You're great kids and I love all of y'all."

Darren stood up and walked over to me, pulled me out of my chair, hugged and kissed me passionately. We were both in tears.

"Ummmmm… excuse me, we are still sitting here," Tyler said.

"Yeah we can see y'all." Demarcus laughed.

Darren and I broke away from our embrace and sat back down.

"I have an idea. Let's take some pictures before our guests arrive," Skylar suggested.

"That's a great idea. Let me go check on Dylan. He should be up by now," Amber said.

"Let's take the pictures in the dining area since it's decorated," I requested.

Skylar went upstairs to retrieve her selfie stick to make our picture taking easy. Amber returned with Dylan dressed and ready for the pictures.

We went into the dining area and took several pictures. Darren and I did a couple of solo poses, the girls did about 50 different poses, Demarcus and Dylan did a few, Darren and the boys, me and the girls and then we did several poses as a group. Every picture was perfect to me because it featured every person who meant the world to me. My family, my blended family; we'd survived so much, and we finally had peace of mind.

If you enjoyed the family drama in the Blended Blessings series, be sure to download CaSandra McLaughlin's next release *Redemption*! Coming Fall 2015!

Chapter 1

Tania Clinton picked up the invitation she'd received in the mail for her baby sister, Naomi's wedding and looked at it again. The parchment paper bore a beautiful yellow and white flower. Simple but cute. Tania hadn't seen her baby sister in years. As a matter of fact she hadn't seen her since she graduated high school and that was ten years ago.

Tania, and Naomi were raised by their oldest sister Mona after their mother Ruby died in her sleep. Tania remembered that day as if it were yesterday.

Tania looked at the invitation again and tears welled in her eyes. She was truly happy for her sister but didn't know if she would be able to attend. Naomi and Tania never had any issues, but she and Mona were like fire and a gas leak; if you got the two of them together, an explosion was bound to happen. Rather than run the risk of ruining Naomi's day, Tania decided she'd buy Naomi a gift and send it to her. She glanced at the invitation again, made a mental note to stop at Wal-Mart later, and tossed the invitation in her desk drawer.

Tania couldn't remember the last time she'd talked to her sisters. Most of her girlfriends bragged about going on trips, shopping sprees, etc. with their sisters. Tania couldn't relate.

Tania had gone to counseling for her issues and her pastor had even told her that she needed to let go and let God. Maybe people who hadn't ever been through anything, who hadn't lost their mothers at an early age, and who didn't have hateful a big sister could let go of things easily. Apparently, Tania's case was a whopper, because for as much as she tried to let go of her old feelings, they wouldn't let go of her.

Tania's thoughts were interrupted by her cell phone. The caller ID let her know it was her favorite cousin, Leslie.

"Hey Leslie, what's going on, girl?"

"What's going on is that I hope you've received your invitation and you plan to come home."

"Yes, I got the invitation but no, I'm not coming home."

"T, why not?" Leslie whined.

"I just don't think it's a good idea."

"I think it's a great idea and it's a great opportunity for you and Mona to get together and bury the hatchet."

"I've buried the hatchet, so I'm good," Tania said, knowing that Leslie wasn't going to give up.

"Look T, I understand your feelings. I really do, but don't you want to make things right? And besides, she's your sister." When the silence on Tania's end went on too long, Leslie blew out an exasperated sigh. "Tania, will you please at least think about it?"

"I've thought about it and I don't want to come. Leslie, you know how Mona is. You've seen her in action."

"Yes, I've seen her in action and I know you don't want to hear this, but I honestly think she has changed."

"Changed what… hairstyles?" Tania said sarcastically.

"Tania, seriously, when she and I talked the other day I was telling her I hoped that you would come home and she said she was excited about seeing you as well."

"That's a first, but I'm still not buying it. Leopards don't change their spots."

"What about the rest of us who want to see you?"

"If the rest of the crew wants to see me, they are more than welcome to mosey on down from Olive, Texas to lil' ole Uhl, Texas to see me. The road travels both ways."

"Girl, ain't nobody got time to be driving to the sticks to see you." Leslie laughed.

"It's peaceful out here in these sticks."

"Anyway girl, I gotta get back to work. Think about what I said and I'll get back with you in a few days."

"Ok, talk to you later," Tania said and hung up the phone.

Leslie's call set Tania back down Memory Lane, which was something she tried her best to avoid doing. But try as she might, Tania could never escape the thoughts. Thoughts about her childhood would creep into her mind and sometimes even her dreams. She had horrible nightmares and often woke up in a sweat. She seriously didn't want to think about Mona, Olive or any of the drama that was attached to her hometown.

But of course she loved her aunt and cousins. She even loved her sisters in some kind of way. She didn't want to be around them for an entire weekend, though.

There was no telling what might happen.

About the Authors

CaSandra McLaughlin is a gospel radio show host who has enjoyed reading and writing for as long as anyone can remember. A native of Marshall, TX, CaSandra loves God, her family, and Mexican food—in that order! *Peace of Mind* is her third book and she looks forward to many more.

Visit CaSandra McLaughlin online at
http://www.facebook.com/casandra.marshallmclaughlin

Michelle Stimpson is the national bestselling author of more than 25 books and 50 short stories. Her work includes the highly acclaimed *Boaz Brown* series, the award-winning *Mama B* series, and the Dafina title *Falling Into Grace*.

Visit Michelle Stimpson online at:
www.MichelleStimpson.com and
www.Facebook.com/MichelleStimpsonWrites

Made in the USA
Lexington, KY
05 March 2017